F
P65   Pintoff, Ernest.
       Zachary.

Temple Israel Library
Minneapolis, Minn.

Please sign your full name on the above card.

Return books promptly to the Library or Temple Office.

Fines will be charged for overdue books or for damage or loss of same.

ZACHARY

About the author

Ernest Pintoff, Academy Award winner for THE CRITIC, is a former animator and film director in motion pictures and TV. Now writing fiction and teaching at the School of Cinema and Television at USC in Los Angeles, Pintoff lives in Hollywood with his wife, Caroline. ZACHARY is his first novel.

A NOVEL

ERNEST PINTOFF

Paul S. Eriksson
PUBLISHER
MIDDLEBURY, VT 05753

Manufactured in the United States of America

10 9 8 7 6 5 4 3 2 1

Library of Congress Cataloging-in-Publication Data

Pintoff, Ernest.
    Zachary: a novel / by Ernest Pintoff.
        p. cm.
    Summary: Sole witness to the grisly murder of a local war hero in a small Connecticut town just after World War II, Zachary joins forces with a big city detective called in to solve the crime.
    ISBN 0-8397-9042-2
    [1. Mystery and detective stories.] I. Title.
PZ7.P635Zac   1990
[Fic]—dc20
                                                            90-37898
                                                                CIP
                                                                 AC

To
dear Caroline

*To conceal a matter, this is
the glory of God,
to sift it thoroughly, the
glory of kings.
High though the heavens are,
deep the earth,
there is no fathoming the
heart of kings.*

PROVERBS

ZACHARY

1

Hitler's suicide marked the end of Nazi terror. And though I rooted for America like we played the Axis in a game of football, I was still glad I didn't have to join in that battle. So many of the hometown guys never even came back. But thoughts of war were not on my mind as I practiced for my upcoming bar mitzvah. I tried on the jacket to my new blue suit, adjusted my necktie and smiled in the full-length mirror behind the bathroom door. On the hexagon tiled floor, my dress shoes were all polished and ready to go.

"My beloved mother, dear brother, Rabbi Glick and good friends . . ."

I could still hear Glick's coaching: "Speak *slowly* and *clearly*, Zachary."

But I continued my own way. "Today, I am a man."

In the reflection, I spotted my brother Lenny's Gillette razor lying conspicuously on the shelf under the medicine cabinet. It was left there no doubt, to remind me that he shaved.

In two weeks I would be delivering my big speech. Then it would be spring and I would be a man. I was aware, of course, that manhood might be more complicated than merely delivering a speech—especially considering all I had been through during the previous months. Springtime used to mean days of baseball, swimming and smoking at Black Rock with my pal, Buddy Goodson. But everything was to change during that winter of '45.

Reaching into my dress shoe, I found the matchbook with "Gino's Eats" on the cover. I still remember Buddy's voice whispering over the phone, "And don't forget to bring matches, Zack." The matches had always been my end, the cigarettes Buddy's. I kept them hidden in the shoe figuring that was the last place my mother would look.

Not long after my twelfth birthday I had started sneaking off with Buddy to light up cigarettes. Mostly, we smoked after a dip in the lake or some one-on-one basketball behind Olaf's Auto Body. It made us feel older, and being strictly forbidden, provided the flash of adventure Oakville, Connecticut sorely lacked. That is, until Mary Beth Porter appeared.

She came to Baldwin Grammar to teach music, painting and drawing—classes I'd always enjoyed. But with Miss Porter, the arts took on a greater dimension. She inspired me to appreciate the beauty of life and love, not to mention the unique design of the female form. And whether I realized it then or not, Miss Porter was probably the most important event in my adolescent life. She was the real reason I became a man. The speech was Glick's idea.

By September, the war had become just another memory, no more important than who was pitching for the Brooklyn Dodgers or what was playing at the Bartlett Cinema. But that first day of the school year was important because it marked the arrival of Miss Porter.

I'll never forget how she appeared in class wearing wedgies and that billowy skirt. I was hooked right off like some hungry bass. After school, Buddy and I tailed her outside and watched as she leaned back against the oak tree behind the gym. Then she smoked two Chesterfields. Over the next week we saw her smoke lots of times—outside during the teacher breaks and before school in her car. It was generally recognized by the boys of Oakville that women who smoked were extra sexy, what with all the big-time movie actresses of the day invariably posed with cigarettes between their shiny lips.

From that first vision, something stirred in my heart that was strange and wonderful. Miss Porter made me feel bigger and bolder and glad as hell I lived in Oakville after all. She even smelled of lilacs, which still remind me of her.

Every day became a challenge. Miss Porter, who had the most beautiful brown eyes and long sandy-colored hair, hardly ever smiled. So Buddy and I vowed to break her up during glee club rehearsals with our sour notes. That was what we lived for, that became our purpose: to wrangle a grin from that gorgeous face. A smile meant victory and celebration, like the winning hit in the World Series.

But even before the first week of classes had ended, rumors were flying that Miss Porter was carrying on with the town cop—who can only be likened to some village ogre from a Grimm's fairy tale. His name was Lewis G. Heinz, but almost everybody called him Big Lew. Actually, Gorilla Lew would've been more appropriate. Besides being the town toughie, Heinz was also the town enigma. No one could fathom how he got the job of "Protector of Peace" in Oakville, not to mention who or what exactly he was protecting, other than his own interests. The thought of a romantic link between Heinz and *any* woman was out of the question, but to imagine something between Big Lew and sweet Mary Beth Porter was laughable. Still, no one could help noticing how Heinz began hanging around Baldwin Grammar more than usual, especially after school when his police car could be seen parked near the teacher's side entrance.

Of course, I suspected that an indiscreet romance was not beyond Miss Porter. It could have been with any one of the poor men she left gasping for breath; Miss Porter was the kind of woman who literally turned heads when she walked down Main Street. But Mr. Bondi, our History teacher, was victim to her flirty charm and breathy sighs every day at close range. So it was no wonder he spent the first week of American History class telling us how Helen of Troy's beauty actually started a war.

Most students liked and admired Bondi, despite his being a lousy teacher. Dark and good-looking like Montgomery Clift, Bondi was famous for his heroic deeds with the U.S. Air Force over Germany. He earned a special medal for being captured, and not only escaping, but returning with valuable maps of enemy munitions dumps. He was the man every boy dreamed of becoming. So whether Bondi could teach history or not was beside the point; he was obviously hired as a role model for the Oakville kids.

By the middle of the second week though, Mr. Bondi had been reduced to just another sniveling boy himself as Miss Porter regularly left him flustered and stammering. Since he was married, I assumed an actual affair was unlikely. What did I know.

One day after school Buddy and I were on our way to Black Rock to share the remains of a pack of Old Golds, the ones with "Apple Honey that helps guard from Cigarette Dryness!" when we heard strange noises from behind the bushes near the playground. I decided to investigate, like some detective on one of those radio crime dramas. Anytime I had the chance to poke into something unusual or odd, I took it. Though I was never sure what I'd find, I secretly hoped it might land me on the front page of the *Waterbury Courier*. As we made our way through the dry grass behind the gym, the noises grew louder.

When thinking about what I saw that day, I can only compare my excitement with the feeling I first had watching Lana Turner in "The Postman Always Rings Twice." That feeling where your body heats up a couple of degrees and you actually start flushing. That was how it was as we watched Bondi caress Miss Porter's breasts and gently ease her back onto the wooden picnic table under the big oak tree. Bondi was huffing and puffing, ready to explode.

Quietly, Buddy and I settled behind the bushes into our front row seats. Neither of us was breathing. Our bodies were stiff and tense. And a trickle of saliva slipped over my lower lip and hit the dirt below. Buddy began slowly rocking back and forth, his bug eyes bouncing around in their sockets like pinballs.

Both of us watched hypnotized as Miss Porter's lipstick-stained cigarette rolled off the table onto the ground where it smouldered in the weeds.

I jabbed Buddy with my elbow as Bondi slipped his hand to her thigh and began to slide her skirt up higher and higher. By now Buddy was wheezing so loudly I thought we'd surely be caught. But Bondi was making more noise than we were, and neither he nor Miss Porter seemed conscious of anything but each other. Then I smelled something burning and noticed the cigarette fizzling in the grass. Buddy wasn't aware of it. His fists were clenched tight at his side and his head tilted back so he could breathe easier. I knew if we made any movement we'd be caught as peepers—and that was certainly not how I imagined making the front page of the *Waterbury Courier*. The smoke soon rose in swirls around the picnic table and surrounded the lovers.

I don't think I'd ever seen sexual contact like that before. It wasn't even the forbidden skin that stirred me. Rather it was the sounds they made which left the impression—the passionate moaning and grunting. Sounds I'd heard only one other time from behind my parents' bedroom door. My pulse was throbbing, my teeth grinding. With Miss Porter's skirt bunched at her waist, Bondi's hand hovered over her black panties like a hawk. Then, as his hand swooped down, Coach Ryan suddenly appeared on the scene with a fire extinguisher. And the moaning and grunting and Buddy's wheezing stopped instantly.

There was a tense, breathless pause before the action started. And we watched Ryan's face as it twitched in growing anger. Finally, in a wild rage, he charged the love-struck couple and tore Bondi off Miss Porter. Like a crazed man, Ryan proceeded to pummel Bondi with flying fists, then with the extinguisher itself.

Buddy, his face all red, shot up and ran like hell. But I couldn't move. I was both excited and terrified. No part of my body would respond; I was frozen. It was like something out of a movie serial or some great radio adventure—and it was happening right in front of my eyes.

With the two men fighting, Miss Porter began screaming hysterically. And within a minute a police siren wailed close from out of nowhere. Frightened for my life, I dove into the bushes for cover.

2

That night after dinner I hardly felt like listening to "Gangbusters" on the radio. As much as I loved that show, where the bad guy always got his due in the end, I'd had enough of murder and mayhem for one day. No word was out yet as to who had killed Bondi. But news spread quickly throughout Oakville that Coach Ryan was being held on suspicion of murder and that Miss Porter had been hospitalized at St. Luke's. I'm surprised the mayor didn't just blab the announcements himself over the old air raid speakers.

Inasmuch as my mother intercepted and monitored all outside communications, there was no way Buddy could get through. She'd already put the phone off limits a few days earlier when she heard us talking dirty. And Buddy was the only one I wanted to speak to about what I'd seen. I knew damn well who killed Bondi, and it wasn't Coach Ryan. But I wondered what had sent Miss Porter to the hospital. She left the murder scene looking troubled, but certainly not harmed. With my brain buzzing, I could barely sleep. And what shut-eye I did get, was filled with strange dreams.

Miss Porter lured me closer with her eyes and that fuming cigarette she held. I obliged, taking a long drag from my cigarette too. And as in every good dream, there was no idle chatter. We just started kissing right then and there. Everything I'd seen Bondi do earlier, I was suddenly acting out myself.

Those were now *my* hands gliding up her silken legs towards those delicate black panties. And those were *my* lips smearing lipstick across that angelic face. But it was also *me* who got caught—standing there with a cigarette in one hand and one of Miss Porter's breasts cupped in the other. Worst of all, it wasn't Coach Ryan who burst on the scene, but my mother. Next thing I knew, I was on trial for nasty behavior and everybody was disgusted with me because I was a disgrace to the honor and innocence of Oakville. Even Buddy was too embarrassed to call me his pal.

As I awoke to the reassuring smell of fresh coffee brewing, I struggled for a brief moment to separate my dream from reality. I wasn't in prison, I was in my own bed, which although lumpy and moist, was better than a cell cot. My father, Bert, always prepared the java, carefully measuring the granules. Then he and my mother, Reva, would pour shots of canned Carnation into their cups and silently have breakfast together, awaiting me and my brother, Lenny.

Getting dressed, I was glad I'd beaten Lenny to the bathroom. With him, everything was a race. Studying myself in the medicine cabinet mirror, I rubbed Brylcreem into my hair, then combed it. Their slogan was ". . . a little dab'll do ya," but I preferred to glop it on for that all-day wet look. At the time, my greatest flaw seemed to be a problem I had with acne—mostly on my forehead. But compared with other kids at school, my complexion resembled a peach. Pushing the tip of my nose with a finger, I tried to imagine how it would look pugged—like Buddy's.

Our boarder, David Maibaum, a graduate of M.I.T. and classified 4-F, worked as a chemical engineer at

Keller Plastic. Quiet and serious, Maibaum lived in the spare room with his boxes of technical books. Those and his bed took up most of the space. Among the numerous things that bugged me about Maibaum was the mechanical way he chewed his food. But he'd already finished breakfast and left for his job by the time I made it into the kitchen. Lenny—his real name was Leonard—was traditionally last to rise. By the time he shuffled in that morning wearing his ridiculous striped shorts and torn undershirt, I was five bites into my French toast.

"No robe?" Bert said, without glancing up.

I was forever amazed by my father's prudishness. He kept his body under wraps and expected the same from everyone else. On the other hand, he thought nothing of peeing in the bathroom without closing the door and often held long conversations with me through the door while he was camped out on the pot.

"You hear what happened?" Lenny announced. "Mr. Bondi got his guts emptied yesterday over at Baldwin."

Neither my father nor I reacted. My mother placed her cup down dramatically. We all knew how Lenny loved to sensationalize. Gruesome, grotesque things fascinated him. Prone to the peculiar, Lenny worked nights at the local bowling alley setting up pins. Even my father occasionally joked that maybe Lenny had taken one bowling ball to the head too many.

"Yeah," Lenny continued, "Bondi copped it right in broad daylight."

My mother, a beautiful, busty woman with intense dark eyes, started to well up. "How could that happen in Oakville?" she said, sobbing. She was like that, always weeping about something. It wasn't Lenny's details that bothered her so much, but what the murder meant: that Oakville wasn't Utopia. Born in strife-ridden Poland, my mother immigrated to America with her folks and sisters when she was a teenager. After she and my father married, they moved from Brooklyn to what they hoped would be greener pastures in Connecticut.

"We heard about the killing at the bowling alley," Lenny said. "Milt Crowell's kid brother saw the body when they were loading it into the meat wagon."

"Okay, that's enough." My father pushed his plate away, then stood and left the kitchen.

I joined him, leaving my mother to hear the rest of Lenny's story. She and Lenny were annoyingly chummy. Primarily because Lenny promised to become a dentist.

"Continue Leonard," my mother urged. Actually, my folks were the only ones he allowed to call him by his real name.

Once during an argument when I addressed him as "Dr. Leonard," he pinned me to the floor and dribbled spit on my forehead until I promised never to call him that again. Lenny had privately admitted to me that dentistry was the last choice on his list and that he was really going to play in a jazz band. I never made any promises to my parents and often wondered if that was why they were forever on my case.

∽✴

As classes had been suspended for the day out of respect for Mr. Bondi, Buddy and I decided to play a little one-on-one behind Olaf's Auto Body. Despite the occasional stench we would catch from the nearby Keller Plastic factory, Olaf's was our favorite place to play because the asphalt there was smooth and level. The hoop was about eight inches low, but the backboard was nice and sturdy. Because the net was usually tattered and clung to the rim by just a few hooks, our first ten minutes were often spent atop piled boxes trying to re-hook it for a few shots before it unraveled again.

Buddy was a fierce competitor in our never-ending sports encounters. What he lacked in quickness, he made up for with distracting chitchat—which he used to give him an edge. One time Buddy even grilled me about a study date I'd had with Evette Labeck.

He harassed me with questions like: "Well, d'ja get a feel?" or "How 'bout yer pecker, did she grab it?" And while I stood there gaping, he slipped around me for the game-winning hoop.

This time though, I was the one more interested in talking than playing. I was shocked that a real war hero like Greg Bondi could suffer such a senseless death; even at age twelve I knew there was something extremely unfair and cruel about that notion.

"The way I see it," I said, dribbling down the baseline, "Ryan must've thought Miss Porter was being attacked by Bondi."

"Aw, c'mon, she was beggin' for it," Buddy grinned.

I sank an easy five footer and was only behind by two.

Buddy kept pumping me. "So what about Big Lew? Where the hell did he come from so fast?"

Buddy always asked tough questions. And I took it as a personal challenge to come up with answers, even if I had to make something up. Taking one off the boards, I proceeded to blow an easy layup. Buddy retrieved it, moved the ball backcourt, picked up his dribble and waited for my reply.

"I guess Big Lew was waiting around for Miss Porter," I said. "Maybe spying on her. Then at the perfect moment, *wham,* there he was!" I just made that up—but it did the trick. "You gotta shoot from there!"

Buddy, unable to dribble, heaved a long shot that missed by a mile. I grabbed the ball and bounced it back out past the foul line. After sinking a set-shot to tie the score, I continued, dead serious. I had Buddy right where I wanted him.

"So you think Big Lew set the whole thing up?"

"I don't know," I said. "But Bondi was out cold when he got there." I looked around to make sure we were alone. Buddy was hanging on every word. "Then Ryan took off with Big Lew right on his ass and went into the trees over by the ballfield."

Buddy looked nervous.

"I was gonna go help Miss Porter," I went on, "because she was shaking and whimpering like a scared puppy." I gave Buddy my best puppy look. "But then Big Lew comes running back, grabs her and tells her to scram. You should've seen her move." Buddy gulped. "So anyway, Big Lew's standing there with his tongue hanging out like a wolf, looking down at Bondi, who's still out cold," I continued. "Then, he takes out this Swiss Army knife that looks like the one Ryan carries around with all the keys and jams it right into Bondi's gut a couple of times, twisting it."

Buddy and I had both grown up fearing and hating Big Lew. He was about six-four, chunked with muscle and a solid beer belly. His thick red neck supported his bristly head. His kind are in countless movies—the cretin who believes might is right. But that Big Lew would actually *kill* someone confirmed our worst fears concerning Oakville's "Protector of Peace."

I watched Buddy's face as it turned white. "Then Big Lew wipes the handle on his pants, chucks the knife in the bushes and takes off back by the ballfield."

Buddy was shaking now. "Then what?"

"Then I ran like hell. Think I'm gonna stick around for a shiv in *my* belly?"

Buddy let the ball drop from his hands then settled on an old truck tire. "I don't feel so hot, Zack."

I could see he was in no shape to continue the game so I sat down next to him and practiced spinning the ball on my finger. But I remember having trouble holding the spin because my hands were trembling.

The one thing I never told Buddy was that after Big Lew took off, I picked up Miss Porter's lipstick-stained cigarette butt, and was keeping it in one of my shoes. That was the only evidence that could tie her to the murder aside from Ryan's word, which I figured, wasn't going to mean much with him in jail.

3

One month earlier—on August 6, 1945 to be exact, the U.S. had dropped the first ever atomic bomb on Hiroshima. On August 9, we unloaded yet another one on Nagasaki. The pictures in the papers and magazines showing the destruction and victims were both frightening and gruesome. But as terrible as they appeared, I believe my chief concern during World War II was that basketballs might be rationed. I had read somewhere that rubber was needed for more important things such as jeep tires and tank treads. That got me thinking that my future as a high school, then college, then pro basketball player might be stifled. But when the war ended, the ball bounced back in my court. And I knew I'd have no excuses for not making the basketball squad.

As the vets started drifting back to town—about a quarter of them had been killed in action—I felt terrible because I'd actually been worrying about sports instead of our boys at war. With the exception of my father, who was working, we all attended a memorial service at Oakwood Fields where an eight man honor guard fired off five salvos. I certainly wasn't the only one with tears in my eyes during the singing of "God Bless America." Then we marched in a long procession along the river bank back to the old Methodist Church.

Oakville, like many old Connecticut industrial towns, edged the Naugatuck River that formed from the surrounding hills and deep springs at Smith's Pond and Black Rock. The winding but gentle river, which practically cut through the entire state, finally empties into Long Island Sound. The railroad ran alongside the river too, crisscrossing over it at different spots. There were two factories in Oakville, both riverside: Oakville Textile and Keller Plastic.

In fifty years Oakville has hardly changed. The town hall, post office and hospital were all built in the early 1900's and still stand to this day. Despite the run-down industrial look of the town, a few picturesque colonial homes and authentic saltboxes have become something of a tourist attraction.

Throughout the long cold winters, Buddy and I used to skate on Smith's Pond next to Keller Plastic playing hockey. The local French Canadian population, large and ever-growing, made winter sports extremely popular. During the war, the textile plant manufactured synthetic fabric for parachutes while Keller Plastic provided a variety of military gadgets and arms parts to the government. But after the war the whole town was talking about reconversion, and half the people employed by Keller were suddenly worried about their jobs.

With nothing quite so pressing on our minds, Buddy and I were on our bikes across the street from St. Luke's Hospital as we watched Big Lew leave the main entrance and slip into a waiting Olds coupe. We couldn't make out who the driver was, though. We both reasoned that Big Lew had just visited Miss Porter. "You think we should drop in and say something to her?"

"Like what," Buddy said, "you got nice panties?"

"No, smartass, like, Are you feeling okay?"

"I don't know," Buddy said. "I gotta get home to clean the dog run."

The Goodson dog run, what with five Irish setters, always needed cleaning.

"Why don't you go see her yourself, Romeo?"

"Aw, forget it," I said. "She probably wouldn't recognize me anyway, her being sick and everything."

Buddy smirked. "Some lover."

I knew he was trying to ride me, so I clipped him on the arm with my fist and took off on my bicycle. Buddy peddled furiously trying to catch up, but his front tire was slightly bent which only made the chase laughable.

It was Buddy who discovered that Heinz had some special arrangement with the local draft board during the war to stay out of the service. Supposedly, he had asthma. But we were convinced it was just an excuse for him to stay in Oakville and continue his reign of corruption and bullying. Either Big Lew was a yellow-belly, I thought, or he wasn't red-blooded. We were always taught that every good citizen wanted to go to war to defend America and return victorious with our flag held high and proud. But after attending the big memorial service, I was grateful that Lenny was a little too young to have served. Not to mention myself. As for Big Lew, I had a hunch he was really just a coward.

At dinner that night my father remarked that everyone in town was talking about the murder. Coach Ryan, who'd been very active in local politics and had been mounting a full-scale campaign to become Oakville's mayor, was doing a lot of squawking from jail. He was insistent that there was no proof of his guilt besides Big Lew's word, which Ryan claimed was "about as reliable as a Nash." It didn't make sense why Miss Porter hadn't said a word about anything. After all, I thought, she knew Ryan took off in the woods before Bondi was knifed. I couldn't understand it.

Since Heinz was both the man Ryan accused of the murder and Oakville's only full-time cop, a detective had to be imported from Waterbury for the investigation. Oakville didn't have its own detective. They'd been stuck for years with Big Lew and his jerk deputies who spelled him during off-hours.

I had already decided not to tell anyone besides Buddy about what had happened. At least not yet. According to my mother, I was always supposed to keep my "nose clean and out of trouble." Those were her rules of life. But this seemed like the most troublesome thing I could get my nose into. Besides, I figured a confession would just bring up too many questions which would have to be answered regarding smoking and spying. Keeping the secret was especially tricky as my mother had a reputation of being the "Queen of Interrogation." Most of all, though, I didn't want to be on this planet when Big Lew found out I had been an eye witness to the murder.

When I was eight, and had finally saved enough nickels and dimes to see "Frankenstein" at the Bartlett, I had my first official run-in with Big Lew. Unknown to me, the theatre had recently been plagued by kids sneaking in and bringing bottles of beer with them. Halfway through the movie—which was frightening enough—someone grabbed me from behind, tore me out of my seat and dragged me out the side exit. For a moment, I thought it was Karloff himself. But when my heart resumed beating and my eyes rolled back to their sockets I was actually relieved to discover it was Big Lew performing a spot check on ticket holders. He threw me against the wall and frisked me viciously, until, in tears, I fumbled out my torn ticket stub. From that day on, I was rightfully terrified of Officer Heinz.

A few years later, Buddy and I had personally witnessed Big Lew beat the living hell out of Chick Popovich after school. Somehow, Heinz had discovered that Popovich broke the window in his patrol car when we were playing hardball the day before. I'll never forget Popovich yelping and bawling as Big Lew roughed him up for what seemed like an hour. After Heinz left, Buddy and I helped Popovich back to his house located in a seedy part of town near the factories. Since no one was home, we just eased the poor guy onto his bed and had to leave him there groaning.

Then there were the stories about Big Lew having killed an out-of-towner who resisted arrest in the parking lot of Gino's Bar and Grill. I was only six years old at the time, but I still remember the sensation it caused. In the end, Heinz's mouthpiece proved the victim had died of a heart attack, and Big Lew was back patrolling the streets.

As much as I hated Heinz, though, I couldn't bring myself to confess what I had seen. I was positive he would kill me and probably my parents too. Then, I figured, some shady lawyer would make it all appear as though Buddy had done it. All I could do was hope with all my heart that everything would somehow be cleared up and that justice would prevail.

"We can't just let Coach Ryan sit in the tank. You've gotta tell what you saw, Zack."

"That's easy for you to say. You've never seen the look in Big Lew's eyes when he's holding a knife."

"I don't know. But if I were you, I'd talk. I mean, who's gonna coach basketball this year if Ryan's stuck in the jug."

I really wanted to tell Buddy he didn't stand a chance of making the squad no matter who was coaching. But I didn't, because he did have a point. I knew it wasn't fair to let Ryan do time when he was totally innocent. Despite his reputation as a hothead, everybody liked Ryan. Or at least they respected his competitiveness. So when he barked, "C'mon kid, get serious!" every young athlete broke his hump to please him. I witnessed ordinary guys tackle hulks twice their weight at Ryan's urgings. I'd even seen little Alan Birdwell hit one over the centerfield fence after Ryan egged him on.

"Maybe you're right," I conceded. "I've just gotta figure out who I'm gonna spill the beans to."

Buddy smiled.

"Hell, the least we could do is stop by and see how he's doing."

"Great idea!"

The Oakville station was a small, shabby precinct house with two holding cells. The lights were dim and the furniture covered with grime. Luckily, Big Lew was out and his newest deputy smiled when I explained that Buddy and I were students from Baldwin who'd come to visit their coach.

Ryan was holed up in the back looking ornery but pathetic through the bars, like some trapped orangutan. Apparently someone had brought his weights, which were neatly stacked on the floor in the corner of the cell. The only thing missing was a rubber tire on a rope.

The moment Ryan saw us, he started right in complaining: "Heinz knows damn well I didn't do anything. He's just trying to kill my campaign. God forbid somebody run this town that doesn't have greased palms."

We'd never heard the term "greased palms" before so the implication was lost on us. Still, I felt that Ryan was glad to see two of his disciples and especially appreciated that we'd brought him peanuts.

"Those were my idea," Buddy informed him.

Ryan grunted his approval. "I tell you I did what any right guy would do when some animal attacks a lady, if that's what you wanna call her," he said, spitting peanut shells onto Buddy's shoes.

I was dying to know what had happened after Ryan leveled Bondi and took off into the trees with Big Lew in pursuit. But I didn't dare ask.

"We know you're innocent," Buddy said. "We'll stand by you."

Ryan crunched away. "I really appreciate that, fellas."

4

Our family store, Silver's General, was located smack in the center of Main Street on the bottom floor of the town's largest building—only three stories high. We lived in the apartment directly over the store, which made going to work in the morning for my father pretty easy. On top of that he got to spend his days with my mother, working hand in hand.

My father was especially proud that my mother had created the store slogan, "We Carry Everything!" which was boldly displayed across the windowfront. "She's wonderful, your mom," he'd boast to me or Lenny, usually when she was well within earshot. My mother loved to be complimented—she needed all the support she could get—and never minded over-hearing the praise. Luckily, my father was happy to oblige.

Silver's sold a variety of cigars, cigarettes and every candy imaginable. We also offered sports gear—bats, balls, sneakers, sox and shirts. In addition to a small soda fountain where we produced fizzy concoctions and chocolate shakes, we sold wine, whiskey and beer—the latter often a cause of embarrassment to me because one of our steadiest customers was Buddy's father. Every day at 5:10 like clockwork, Mr. Goodson—blue-veined nose glowing—would stop by the store for his customary bottle of wine and six-pack. I didn't know why exactly, but I was uneasy

23

about Buddy's father seeing me and usually hid behind a counter when he came in.

Silver's General was a local household name, and we had a thriving business. Those in the know, however, were well aware that although my father called himself the owner, it was my mother who made all the big business decisions—he was tops with the ice cream scoop but she was the shrewd one. Her aggressiveness was always a bit strong for my taste, which probably explains why I liked Melissa Edwards, the pretty, shy Irish girl who lived in the apartment above ours.

Melissa was pleasantly compliant; she'd sit on the back wooden steps tirelessly watching me toss a tennis ball against the stairs while coyly opening and closing her legs. Our friendship was probably the only thing I kept from Buddy. For instance, I never told him that Melissa, who was in our class, often let me copy her Math and Latin homework. I knew if Buddy caught wind of that, we'd surely have to shoot freethrows for her. And if there was one thing Buddy was good at, it was freethrows. But for some reason, Melissa and I chose to keep a mostly low-profile love affair going, relying on unspoken words, flushed cheeks and meaningful eye contact.

Since walking Melissa to school was a breach of our silent understanding, I usually met Buddy outside his house on the way to Baldwin. That next morning was no different, except that Buddy was waiting for *me*—which always meant that he had something very important to say.

Buddy, who had an opinion on everything, reported that it was "hate at first sight" between Big Lew and the detective they brought in from Waterbury. "And I bet there's gonna be a fight, too," Buddy predicted.

Of course, there was nothing to back up that claim. Buddy had somehow coaxed the info from his father, a V.P. for Connecticut Utilities who had access to all the inside town gossip. I realized that the news was questionable at best, though, because Mr. Goodson was usually soused. Buddy even admitted that his old man was drinking more than ever lately and had taken to belting him for no particular reason. Mr. Goodson had also started taking swipes at Mrs. Goodson, who was understandably terrified of him. Buddy said he was thinking of throwing a punch at his father if he kept up with the slugging. And since Buddy was getting bigger, I knew a storm was brewing. Still, looking on the bright side, whenever Mr. Goodson came home, if Buddy was around, they'd actually get out into their driveway and shoot a few hoops together. My father just never had the time, not to mention the inclination.

Apparently Mr. Goodson had tied one on the night before and told Buddy's mother that Heinz informed the mayor he'd be forced to resign if he had to start "taking crap from some goddamn outside Jew cop."

I grinned at the thought. "He's Jewish?"

"Yeah, didn't I tell you that?"

"Nope."

"Well, he's Jewish. And you know what a bigot Big Lew is. Hell, I don't need to tell ya."

I'd been called "Jewboy" several times by Heinz,

tempting me to return the favor by calling him "Fathead!" Fortunately, I just lowered my head and walked away.

That day at school during recess we were introduced to the new detective. My first impression was that he was too easygoing and short to be an effective cop, especially if he was going to tangle with Big Lew. His name was Lieutenant Harry Roth and he looked like John Garfield, but he had a slight European accent. He was soft-spoken and seemed intelligent—something you couldn't say about Oakville's finest. Roth didn't talk down to the kids, either. Instead, he told the class that he'd be speaking to each of us personally within the next forty-eight hours. Then he made the mistake of asking if anyone had any questions. I just knew it would be embarrassing when Birdwell's hand shot up.

"How can you be a real police officer 'n chase crim'nals with a stupid limp?" he said.

I expected the lieutenant to redden with embarrassment. But instead, he remained completely calm. "To be honest, most of my work entails listening, thinking and talking to people," Roth said. "Chasing criminals isn't my department."

I shot a look over at Buddy. He didn't seem too sure about Roth either. The truth was, I'd been hoping Oakville would inherit an untouchable, not some little runt who did mostly "listening, thinking and talking." I had visions of a humdinger brawl though, when and if Roth ever had to square off against Big Lew.

Finally Roth admitted to the kids that in addition to a slight limp, his right hand was impaired, "the result of a shooting incident following a big bank robbery." And that he was still practicing firing with his left hand.

Birdwell had another question. "Is that stupid hand why you didn't go in the army?"

Roth coolly explained that as the sole breadwinner in his household and father of young twins, he was exempted. But Birdwell didn't buy it. He made an annoying little grunt, then took off, his point more than made.

✥

Generally, my routine after school used to start with a snack, either at home or at the store. Being the son of folks who owned Silver's General I had a privileged selection of assorted goodies. If Melissa was around after school, I'd treat her to anything she wanted while my mother was tied up with customers. Sometimes, though, my mother would try to unload some new confection which we'd have to take outside and pawn off on the first mutt dumb enough to come running. I never really cared for my mother's cooking either, with the possible exception of her potato pancakes. That's why I developed the habit of smothering everything she made with ketchup: sandwiches, soup, casseroles, spaghetti and eggs. Anything that wasn't sweet. As long as it ended up tasting like ketchup, I could stomach my mother's meals. Ketchup was far and away my favorite food—even though, according to Buddy's old man, Heinz claimed that *his* grandfather actually invented the stuff. But I chose not to believe that in light of Mr. Goodson's uncertain credibility. Besides, that surely would've ruined the taste for me.

If Melissa wasn't around, I would wander over to Buddy's for a snack where I was guaranteed to find some great cookies or cake. Buddy's mother was probably the best cook in town, which partially explained Buddy's size. My favorite was her Boston Cream Pie. Buddy's mother sprinkled bits of semi-sweet chocolate on the top and served huge slices.

Between snacktime and supper I usually perused the *Waterbury Courier*. As Oakville was too small to have its own newspaper, we got all the newspapers from Waterbury, the nearest big city. The *Courier* carried Dick Tracy and Li'l Abner among others. My favorite, Tracy, was always involved in exciting adventures—yet always managed to keep his cool. I had hoped Roth would be like Tracy—some super-hero who'd swoop into Oakville and clean up the town. Tracy was fun to sketch, too. He was easy to copy, with those angular features and hatchet-like nose. Whenever troublesome things were on my mind, I would sketch the events in my life. Often, Tracy would wind up in the drawings with me and Buddy, helping us break some undercover spy ring. I loved drawing because I could create my own little world where people like Tracy and I worked to-gether, using our wrist-radios and other gizmos to battle the forces of evil. I realized, however, that I couldn't fight Big Lew with a pencil.

Sprawled on the rug in the living room, I'd been enjoying Tracy's latest cartoon exploits, that is until

Lenny appeared. "Big Lew stopped me after school today," he said. Lenny, who attended Oakville High, had also been indoctrinated with Officer Heinz's viciousness since he was a little kid. "You'll never guess," Lenny grinned. "He wanted to know where you were when Bondi got knifed. And he had that look in his eye like maybe he wanted to get you alone for a little grilling."

My stomach knotted. I hated the way Lenny dramatized things. "What was he asking about me for?"

"You tell me," Lenny said.

"Did he really wanna know where I was?"

Lenny wouldn't answer. Instead, he slapped me on the head, then wandered into the kitchen.

I prayed Lenny was just trying to get me going. But I was scared as hell regardless. What if Big Lew had already discovered I was the only witness?

Even though we lived on the second floor with no access except the front door and back door through the store, I wasted no time locking all the apartment windows.

5

My biggest gripe was about my family. I wanted someone kinder than Lenny as a brother, someone smarter, to look up to and idolize. And I wanted a mother like Mrs. Goodson, a mother who doted on me and baked fresh pastries all the time. Ideally, my father would've been like Charlie Chan, with me as his number one son helping him on all the tough cases. It wasn't that I felt mistreated or neglected. I simply longed for something more than I had, something better. Buddy, on the other hand, regularly wished he was *me* with free rein over Silver's General and folks too busy to checkup on him all the time. But when you're a kid, taking things for granted is part of your job.

Sitting under the elm tree across the street from the Goodson house, I waited impatiently for Buddy. I figured he was having another one of those big morning meals—with bacon, sausages and eggs. At my house, I was lucky to get cinnamon toast. Still, I realized that a hearty breakfast wasn't worth all the guff he had to take.

I watched Mr. Goodson climb into his Studebaker, back out of the driveway and zigzag off to work—thanks, no doubt, to the gin kicker in his grapefruit juice. Next came Buddy's younger sisters, Claire and Pam, who skipped out of the house together and made their way towards school. Claire already had budding breasts and enjoyed playing football with the boys, often providing me a quick feel in the pileup. Mrs. Goodson had once asked me to take Claire to the movies, and although I liked Claire, I flushed anxiously and concocted some feeble excuse about a contagious ear infection. Actually, the thought of being seen with ten-year-old Claire posed serious problems for my reputation.

When Buddy finally appeared, his mother handed over his bagged lunch and gave him a big kiss goodbye. Those were the kind of things that always made me jealous. I had to make my own lunch, throwing together a sandwich with whatever scraps were left behind by the two resident hyenas, Lenny and Maibaum. And there was certainly no fanfare when I took off for school. In fact, I usually left the apartment unnoticed, without even so much as a simple "So long" or "Good luck."

I'd been waiting impatiently for Buddy because I had a few questions. Namely, I wanted to find out what was behind Big Lew's sudden curiosity about me. As far as I was concerned, Buddy was the only person who knew where I was that afternoon of the murder.

"You always blame me," Buddy said.

"Well *I* sure as hell didn't say anything."

"Lemme think," Buddy said, as we trudged towards school. "Maybe you should talk to Popovich."

"What the hell does *he* know?"

"Didn't I already tell you?"

I sighed. Typically, Buddy had not said one word about Popovich before now.

"He was the one who gave me the Old Golds," Buddy said. "Popovich had to stay after school that afternoon. Anyway, I caught him just before he took off. Lucky for us, huh?"

It wasn't easy to locate Popovich because he never hung around with classmates. He was fourteen, bigger than most high school sophomores, never washed his hair and was covered head to toe with pimples, prompting some older students to call him "Pockovich." Most of the kids in our class however, were scared of him, not necessarily because he bullied them—the potential was there, though, and went a long way in dictating our fears. Popovich had already repeated seventh grade three times, which said all there was to know about his intelligence. Nevertheless, Buddy and I were duly impressed with the way he folded his cigarette pack under the sleeve of his T-shirt.

I finally found him sitting alone in back of the bleachers dragging on a butt and carving something in the wooden supports. "Hiya Chick. Mind if I ask you something?"

"You just did," he said with an amused snort and blast of smoke from his nose.

I grinned, but decided to push on with my inquiry anyway. "Has Big Lew asked you anything lately?"

Popovich looked at me suspiciously. "He sure the dick did. Ryan told him I skipped P.E. and was on detention sweepin' the gym, so 'Big Loser' grilled me about the murder, wanted to know everything I saw."

"What'd you say?"

"I told him I saw a lot of crap aroun' so I cleaned it up." He laughed at his lame joke again.

"Did you happen to mention me or Buddy?"

"Sure the dick did. I told him Goodson was

around, and getting rounder everyday!'' He guffawed again, then folded up his pocketknife. ''But I didn't say nothin' to that little Waterbury gimp when *he* started nosin' around.'' Popovich liked to talk tough, though I knew if anyone in authority pressured him enough, he'd fold like any other kid.

I sat through the rest of my classes secretly writing down every detail of the recent events. All my attention was focused on the murder now. School, sports and girls would have to take a back seat. I had a special interest in this case—my life.

After school I tried to piece together the whole story for Buddy as I saw it. ''Ryan wanted to let Roth know that he wasn't the only one around.''

''So he tells him about Popovich,'' Buddy added, trying to make like a detective too.

''And Popovich tells Big Lew about you,'' I said.

''Me?'' Buddy squeaked, his face going red.

''Yeah, but that probably means me, too. So *that* explains his snooping around and asking Lenny about me.''

Realizing he wasn't in this mess alone, Buddy looked smug, almost smiling. ''Damn, this is exciting.''

And in a sickening way, it was. Though I didn't admit as much.

∞

On Sunday nights my favorite radio show was ''The Jack Benny Program.'' Lenny and I, and our folks—if they weren't too busy—would gather in the living room to soak up all the antics from our big Emerson console.

The bit I liked best on that show was when a holdup man would say to Benny, "Your money or your life!"

Benny, the tightwad, would wait forever to answer, causing the studio audience to first snicker, then cackle, and finally roar with delight. When the laughter subsided, the robber would repeat his demand. And Benny would wait several seconds longer—then bring the house down with his annoyed reply: *I'm thinking! I'm thinking!*

That night, despite Benny's indelible humor, I still had trouble sleeping. My fear of Big Lew was beginning to take a terrible grip on me. I closed my eyes and prayed that if Big Lew ever confronted me, I'd at least have the option of giving up my money for my life.

∾⋆

On Monday morning I spotted Miss Porter as she strolled into the teachers' lounge. She seemed fine—a little sullen, but still sexy as ever. I could hardly wait to see her in class because I'd made a "Welcome Back" card for her. It had a drawing of me and Buddy in goatees, top hats and tails, holding open the doors to Baldwin Grammar. Whenever I drew myself I naturally pictured a man, not a boy. Whether it was a goatee or a full beard, I always found some way to make myself look older. Even in conversation, I added a year or so to my age when possible. I especially liked to borrow Lenny's high school band jacket to beef up my image.

Upon seeing the "Welcome Back" card, Buddy immediately complained that he looked "goofy." But I convinced him the idea behind that was to make Miss Porter smile.

"Yeah, yeah," he said. "But why'd you have to draw my shoes so big? I look like Bozo!"

"You said it," I teased, "not me." This, of course, earned me a swift sock to what eventually, I would call a bicep.

During recess, playing touch football, we noticed Miss Porter talking with Big Lew at the far end of the field. The wind was gently blowing her hair and those gorgeous legs were silhouetted beneath her breezy skirt. Big Lew was in uniform and, as usual, his shirt looked about two sizes too small. The squad car was parked behind them with that enormous number 17 stenciled on the door. I didn't have a clue why it was that number, since Oakville had only one car in its illustrious squad.

"I thought Big Lew was off the case," Buddy remarked.

"Same here," I said, still staring over at them and I decided not to pursue the loose ball which had bounced in their direction. Instead, we watched Popovich reluctantly retrieve it.

We continued playing until the school bell sounded. Starting back inside, I noticed Big Lew pull Miss Porter close to him. She squirmed, then pecked his puffy cheek.

"Why couldn't it have been Big Lew that got the knife in his gut."

"With *his* belly it wouldn't a done much damage," Buddy smirked. While we got our books for the next class, he said: "I've been thinking. We gotta get our story straight before Roth gets us alone."

I'd been diligently avoiding the thought. Although I was convinced the truth was entirely out of the question, I wasn't the smoothest liar, either. The worst part was, there was no adult to talk it over with. Lenny would never have understood, and I knew Maibaum wouldn't want to get involved. Worst of all, if my parents found out I would have been locked away in my room for eternity.

"Just don't spill anything to this guy Roth," I told Buddy. "I'll figure out something."

6

Lieutenant Harry Roth drove a '41 Packard, and as he was working more or less undercover, the car became his office. For security reasons, I assume, Roth spoke to us individually in "The Pack" after school. By the time it was my turn to speak with him, I remember my palms being telltale moist. So when he greeted me with an extended hand, I opted for a friendly nod instead.

Since it was the first time I'd ever been in a Packard, I carefully took in all the details: the green two-tone upholstery with vinyl trim, the long sleek dash with convex dials. There was also a tiny star of David dangling on a slender chain from the rearview mirror.

Roth appeared a lot more relaxed than when he first spoke to our class but all I could do was sit there and stare outside as the rain splattered off the windshield. I could barely make out Buddy who was anxiously waiting for me under cover of a huge maple tree across the street.

"You cold?" Roth asked, offering a blanket he withdrew from behind the car seat.

I tried to stop my hands from shaking, not sure if it was the cold vinyl seatcover or my nerves. "No, I'm okay."

"Good." Then his eyes met mine. "I understand you and Buddy were around school at the time of the murder."

I squirmed in my seat.

"You'd better tell me everything you know," he said, grinning slightly. "'Cause a good detective'll find out sooner or later."

Having listened to my share of radio crime dramas, I knew he was right.

"I'm afraid the man we're dealing with here is capable of horrendous brutality," he said. "But I can help you, Zachary," Roth continued. "If you know something, you've got to tell me. A man's life is at stake here."

All I could think was, "So is mine!"

"You can trust me," he said, "if that's what you're worried about."

The phrase, "trust me," has never impressed me. And at the time, I was damned if I was going to tell some strange cop that I'd witnessed a cold-blooded murder by a lunatic who could easily do the same butcher job on me. Besides, I was determined to protect Miss Porter; it seemed like the heroic thing to do. So I decided to keep everything between just me and Buddy. From the way Roth was talking, though, I wondered if Buddy hadn't already spilled the beans.

"The truth of the matter is," I said, looking away, "that afternoon, Buddy and I went over to Black Rock after school."

"Oh?" Roth said. "What'd you do there?"

"Promise not to tell my parents?"

"You can count on me."

"We went there to smoke."

Roth relaxed. "What brand?"

"Old Golds," I said proudly.

Roth grinned and nodded. I suddenly felt a great deal more comfortable, shifting my gaze from the little star of David back to him.

"I want you to know that you can always come to me if you want to talk man-to-man, Zachary."

⟋⋊

Every weekday night after dinner The Silver household tuned into the radio news by Gabriel Heatter. During the war we couldn't have missed more than one or two of his broadcasts on MBS. My father always got a kick out of the way I mimicked Heatter's show opener: "Ah, there's good news tonight!" But that night I was in no mood for parlor games.

The newscaster talked about the Nazi leaders who had committed suicide or tried to disguise and hide themselves after the war's end. Apparently, many of the high-ranking officers carried cyanide tablets with them at all times just in case they were discovered.

"What's cyanide?"

Before my father could answer, Maibaum paused mid-dessert and started spouting: "Cyanide is a substance composed from the cyanogen group," Maibaum licked his lips and continued "which, when combined with potassium or sodium, yields a highly toxic chemical capable of arresting the heart within fifteen seconds after entering the bloodstream." Pleased with himself, Maibaum grinned and leaned back in his chair.

No doubt my father was relieved. But he sipped his coffee with a disinterested look, like Maibaum hadn't said anything he didn't already know.

As Lenny and I washed and dried the dishes, I pondered the murder. Why did Heinz kill Bondi? Was he jealous? That *had* to be the answer. Heinz was jealous of Bondi and Miss Porter. But I wondered if she had any idea Heinz was Bondi's killer. After all, she took off *after* Ryan attacked Bondi. If she did know, though, I figured Big Lew would be forcing her to keep quiet, probably borrowing a few concentration camp torture tricks from the Nazis.

Buddy and I often considered the presence of Nazis in Oakville. When the war first started we used to imagine that several sinister-looking characters in town were prominent figures of the Third Reich. I wasted no time forming a secret team to search for enemies, and we actually spent an entire day once making badges out of tin foil and listing all the possible Nazis we'd track down. Along with a couple of Canadian high school seniors who used to terrorize us at Smith's Pond, we put Big Lew high on our list of possible Gestapo officers. But as soon as the baseball season arrived, we gave up those plans and decided to work on our batting averages. My greatest ambition at the time was to hit like Joe DiMaggio—even though he wasn't a Dodger.

After my family had turned in for the night, I slipped down the back stairs into the store and helped myself to a glass of milk browned with U-bet fountain chocolate syrup. I'd already decided to forego translating my Latin assignment on the Roman

Legions, figuring I could cop it from Melissa in the morning before class. What I needed was the comfort of a drawing tablet.

With the pad propped on my knees, I sketched out all the characters involved in the crime. I drew Heinz twice the size of Bondi and Ryan. Next to Big Lew, I sketched in Mr. X. That's what I called the stranger who drove off with Big Lew from the hospital. I shaded him in like a shadow. But I was having difficulty drawing Roth. I kept making the lieutenant tougher-looking than he really was. Scribbling away, I couldn't stop wondering what Roth meant when he said this case was "much more important" than I could imagine. I finally gave up trying to draw him and tore out the page, stashing it with the rest of the sketches under my bed.

Before turning off the light I made sure the door to my room was shut tight. Then I went into the closet, retrieved my right dress shoe and sat back down on the bed. Reaching into the most secret hiding place I owned, I carefully extracted the lipstick-stained cigarette butt and sniffed, trying to recall Miss Porter's lovely scent. But all I could smell was dried-out tobacco. Returning the evidence to the shoe, I flicked the light off and snuggled under the covers, my mind still spinning.

The dream started off slowly this time. I had just seen a photograph of Heinz reduced to ashes in her fireplace. Now I was in the bedroom and the light was low. There was no crime to solve, just a perfect moment to share as she approached from the shadows in her black satin negligee. Everything was happening in slow-motion, giving me plenty of time to enjoy the vision. Passing me a cigarette still wet from her full lips, Miss Porter winked slyly.

"Chesterfields," I murmured, mimicking the ad slogan. "They satisfy."

She was amused by my sophisticated wit, giggling and gazing into my eyes. It was obvious she wanted a kiss. But as I moved towards her, her mouth swelled with a redness that oozed down her face. Suddenly her eyes glazed over and her body went limp. Groping for my arm, she fell to the floor. There was a Swiss Army knife stuck deep in her back.

7

It wasn't that I didn't like David Maibaum, it's just that I never got a say in whether we took in a boarder. My mother, forever plotting ways to generate extra income, decided on her own to accept Maibaum as a lodger during the war. Even my father and Lenny were opposed to the idea, but that didn't seem to count. She explained that taking David in was not only financially wise, but it was also "honoring a request" by Sol Keller, owner of Keller Plastic. Keller, who was "Mr. Influential" in Oakville, had been awarded a plaque by the U.S. Department of Defense for his contribution to the war effort. And since he was such an "outstanding citizen," as my mother's reasoning went, the honor was really ours.

After yet another bad dream, I got up earlier than usual and managed to catch Maibaum before he left for work. A cursory "morning, Zack" was all he could muster. Dressed in the same woolly cardigan as always, Maibaum was just about to dig into his Quaker Oats. He had that every morning rain or shine, along with sliced fruit, sugar and cream.

"You look troubled, Zachary." Maibaum's tone was formal, stilted. "What's on your mind?"

"I guess this murder thing's got to me."

He straightened, wiping a blob of cereal from his lips. "The whole factory's buzzing. You should hear their crazy theories."

You should hear the *truth*, I thought, as I poured myself a glass of pineapple juice from the can in the fridge. My mother always pushed juice in the morning, saying it was "good for digestion." We went through phases: tomato juice one week, apple the next. But my favorite, Dole's Pineapple Juice, was forever on hand.

"I've got my own theory," Maibaum said. He moved to the sink and rinsed out his bowl. "I've got a feeling this is something really strange, something a heckuva lot bigger than some little murder. I can just feel it."

I knew all about Maibaum's feelings. If he had a feeling it would rain, he'd trudge off to work in slicker and rubbers. If he had a feeling he was going to catch cold, he'd suck on citrus fruit all day.

My father, already dressed, appeared and automatically went for his trusty packet of Chase and Sanborn.

"Guess what?" I said. "Dave's got a feeling the Bondi murder's 'really strange.' "

Maibaum blushed.

"Strange, huh?" My father, who worked long hours, looked half-asleep as he tried to fill the aluminum percolator with the exact amount of water. "Well, I'll bet Dave's right this time."

Maibaum's grin was short-lived. "I've also got a terrible feeling I'll be getting laid off soon," he said.

Almost every day without fail, Maibaum worried about his job. My father liked to joke that if Dave had a nickel for every second he worried, he'd be a Rockefeller and would never have to work again. "Let's hope you go one for two on these feelings of yours," my father said, still attempting to get the water level right in the percolator.

"I'll settle for that," Maibaum said. He finally departed, mumbling "Goodbye" while I prepared my breakfast.

"No cream?" My father, obviously upset, was peering into the fridge—he couldn't tolerate his coffee black, and we were out of Carnation. It was always a battle as to who would skim the cream off the top of the milk first. And since Maibaum was earliest to rise, he had first dibs.

"Dave used it for his oatmeal," I said, fully expecting my father to get that we-never-should've-taken-in-a-boarder scowl. He didn't disappoint.

◦✗

I began to notice that things were changing between Buddy and me. We didn't share as much time together anymore and the few hours we did were usually spent discussing Lieutenant Roth and the Bondi murder, which seemed to disturb Buddy more than it did me.

"How come you trust Roth anyway?" Buddy asked sarcastically, " 'Cause he's Jewish?"

I rolled my eyes. "No," I said. "I trust him 'cause he's got a .38."

"So what? My father's got a .22 and a whole box of shells I can use any time I want."

I'd never seen Buddy so jealous. But that was part of why I liked him: he was so competitive. It actually made me try harder in sports *and* school. I just hated to get beaten by Buddy in anything. And he was the same way. That's why we were best friends. Looking back on it, I'm sure Buddy felt like an outsider with both me and Roth being Jews—this struck me as peculiar even then as *we* were the outsiders. There were only two Jewish families in town: us, the Silvers, Polish-Russian ghetto descendants, and the Kellers, German Jews. Buddy was Catholic like mostly everybody else in Oakville.

"Bet you gotta go to Hebrew School today, huh?" Buddy remarked.

Three times a week since July, I'd been taking the bus to Hebrew School at the old orthodox Temple Beth Zion in Waterbury to prepare for my upcoming bar mitzvah. "You got it, Buddy."

"Boy, I wish I was Jewish," he grumbled. "At least I'd have something to do after school."

Hebrew School was something akin to prison. About six months before my thirteenth birthday, my parents decided it was time I began learning Hebrew. Not only did I have to spend forty-five minutes traveling to and from Waterbury in broken-down, stuffy buses, but sitting in that dark and dingy synagogue for a two hour lesson was hardly my idea of afterschool fun. And I was convinced that my teacher, Rabbi Glick, had singled me out for persecution.

We were forced to read boring books written in Hebrew and listen to Glick drone, for what seemed like days, on the significance of being Jewish. I understood that the main purpose of Hebrew School was to prepare bar mitzvah boys for manhood, but that was a problem for me. In my mind I already *was* a man. And if I wasn't yet a man, I figured it was just a matter of time; reading those books and hearing monotonous lectures was certainly not going to speed up the process. As luck would have it, I was usually able to smuggle in a couple of comic books and a scratch pad to help while away the time. If only Buddy knew what he was missing.

"Well I sure hope Roth can shoot with that dumb hand of his. 'Cause if Big Lew finds out you're a witness, he's gonna have a pink fit," Buddy warned. "Fact, I wouldn't be surprised if he showed your belly that knife of his."

"Big Lew won't find out. And I'm not telling Roth anything."

"Bullshit!"

"Bullshit yourself! Besides, if I wanted to talk, we'd probably end up working on the case together."

"And Harry Truman wants me to take over for General MacArthur," Buddy shot back. "You're such a sap, Zack. Roth wants to use you just so he can get some promotion for himself. I mean, why else would he bother with you?"

He had a point, although I would never have admitted it.

When I got home later, I was more than surprised to find Roth's Packard parked outside our apartment. And as I started to unlock the front door I could hear my mother and the detective chuckling inside.

"Zachary," my mother greeted. "Lieutenant Roth told me that you two have already met."

I placed my books on the little table in the foyer and joined them. They were having tea and honey cake.

"Guess what?" my mother said.

"What?"

"The lieutenant is from Poland, too. Vilna."

Roth looked up from his tea and grinned.

"His father," she continued, "was a very famous Jewish scholar." My mother was noticeably impressed. "The lieutenant comes from a very respected Yiddish family," she said. "Normally I'd be nervous about you speaking with a detective," she smiled. "But I know you're in good and safe hands."

Roth sipped his tea and gazed at me. I didn't care how 'good and safe' his hands were, Big Lew's hands were bigger and stronger. The better to wring a kid's neck.

"Here, Lieutenant," my mother said, lifting the platter of goodies she'd brought out. "Have some more honey cake."

I took a piece of cake too. When my mother left us alone, Roth placed his teacup down and looked directly into my eyes.

"Now are you *sure* you didn't notice anything strange or unusual that day after school?"

Despite Roth's grilling, I kept mum. In a way, he seemed impressed by my strength. Still, I could tell he wasn't completely buying my story. And it occurred to me that if I did decide to talk, maybe I could become his "partner," regardless of what Buddy said. Maybe listening to all those radio crime shows was going to pay off.

After he left, my mother explained that Roth thought I was a "bright kid," and merely wanted to ask me a few questions about school. I smiled, knowing that he already pulled one over on her. I liked his style, but I knew my father would never be so trusting.

8

Every autumn I looked forward to winter and another season of hockey on Smith's Pond. All my favorite players in the NHL were small, compact and speedy. Granted I was still on the gangly side, but I was quickly becoming a better skater as my legs grew stronger.

I had been planning for weeks to buy a new hockey stick with the money I'd saved doing odd jobs over the summer. So as the school bell sounded, Buddy and I piled out of the Boys' Entrance along with all the other guys. The weekend was before us.

"How 'bout a little skating, Bud?"

"Forget it," he said. "You're busy."

"What are you talking about? Today's Friday." Fridays meant no Hebrew School.

Buddy smirked, and pointed to the Packard parked across the street. We continued toward the wooden rack which housed our bikes, and I noticed the passenger door of the '41 sedan swing open, beckoning. I could make out the lieutenant eyeballing me from behind the wheel. Obviously Roth wanted to talk.

"See ya later, deputy." Buddy took off. I crossed the street and climbed into the car. Roth greeted me with a grin. "No basketball today?"

I gave him a look. "Me and Buddy were . . ."

"Personally," Roth interrupted, "I like N.Y.U. this year."

I was surprised he even knew they had a basketball team.

"Would you believe I played freshman ball for N.Y.U.?" Roth said. "But I was too short to make varsity. It's tough for little guys these days." He paused and gazed towards the school. "DePaul's got a player this year named Mikan. The guy's *six-nine!*"

I knew damn well how tall Mikan was. "I hope that isn't what you wanted to talk about," I said.

He chuckled, but quickly turned serious. "As a matter of fact, I had an interesting chat with Ryan this morning."

Just then I noticed Melissa walk by with an armful of books. I realized I hadn't spoken to her since the murder. Melissa looked pretty with her ponytail bouncing over her kelly green sweater. And her cheeks were rosy from the Connecticut chill. I wanted to hop from the Packard and roll her in the snow like I'd done so many times before, but my life was becoming more than a casual exercise in school, sports and girls. No longer was growing up a simple matter of just getting out of bed each morning, which was all that had previously been required of me.

"Ryan claims that after finding Bondi messing around with Miss Porter, he decked him," Roth said. "Then before he knew it, Ryan heard a siren, panicked, and ran off."

I restrained myself from confirming Ryan's story.

"Of course," Roth said, "I've got no proof about Miss Porter. So I'll have to interrogate her myself."

"Yeah," I said, not thrilled with that prospect.

"She seems like such a sweet person," Roth said. "I can't imagine her mixed up in this thing. What do you think?"

"Me neither," I remarked, wondering what shade of crimson my face was.

"Ryan also claims that after Heinz caught him and cuffed him to a tree, Heinz stole his Swiss Army knife and disappeared for five minutes."

I tried to appear only vaguely interested.

"Frankly," Roth said, "I don't believe Ryan killed Bondi"

I thought about that for a few moments. "Then how can you let him sit in jail if he's innocent?"

"Ryan knows what the situation is. I explained everything to him this morning. But it's not *him* I'm worried about," Roth said, staring out the windscreen. "I really don't want to get you involved in this thing. But I think you should know something, Zachary." He watched my eyes to measure my reaction. "We think Heinz could be connected to the Nazi party."

I was stunned, although I really didn't understand exactly what that meant.

"The reason I'm telling you this is that if you've been keeping something from me, now's a good time to speak up. There's a lot more at stake here than just your coach spending his holidays in jail."

I'd heard all about Nazi tactics: the extreme cruelty, starvation and brainwashing. Suddenly Big Lew became ten times as terrifying, and I was overcome by visions of myself being hunted down and tortured until I confessed everything I knew. It was Nazi against Jew. "I thought the damn war was over."

By this time, most of the kids had disappeared and some of the teachers began leaving.

"Officially, yes," Roth said. "But there're still a few outstanding matters which have to be dealt with."

I could see Miss Porter leaving the school building looking slightly frazzled as she made her way to a coupe parked curbside. The car looked familiar. She hesitated, then entered the auto with the help of an extended hand from the back seat. Before the door was closed, the coupe roared away. Roth, who'd been wiping his windscreen with a hanky, didn't notice the incident.

"When I was sixteen," he said, reminiscing, "my father sent us to America. Just my mother and me. And we didn't speak a word of English. The plan was he was going to join us later." Roth took a deep breath. "But plans have a funny way of not working out the way you want."

"What happened?"

Roth swallowed hard. "He never got out. They murdered him less than a year ago in the Holocaust."

"I'm sorry," I said, not knowing what else to say.

Roth appeared deeply affected. "I don't know if I can ever forgive the Germans," he said. "Not just for Papa, but for everything and everyone they destroyed."

9

Weekends had a way of cleaning the slate between Buddy and me. Sunday night I'd made a vow to change my life, to get back to the basics: sports and girls. So on Monday when Buddy suggested we play touch football after school then go to his place for some of his mother's caramel apples, I agreed without hesitation. Pretty soon everything was back to normal and he was ribbing me about the Dodgers' rotten chances for a pennant victory. Knowing that Brooklyn was my favorite team, it was his way of getting to me. My only defense of the "Bums" was Dixie Walker's hitting, which had been nothing short of sensational.

"But how 'bout Basinsky?" Buddy reminded. "He's suckin' eggs." No argument there. Eddie "The Violin" Basinsky, a wartime fill-in player for Brooklyn, was just completing yet another lousy season. "Any dummy can tell from Basinsky's batting average," Buddy teased, "that he can't hit fer shit."

Though it was tough to concede, Chicago, Buddy's heroes, were on their way to whipping Detroit in the World Series. Buddy firmly believed that the Cubs' good fortune had something to do with his undying support.

After a long, hard day of English, Biology, Algebra and Latin, we relished our final class in the Art Room with Miss Porter. And when she asked me to help clean up after school I almost strained my neck nodding too fast. Glancing over at Buddy, I was slightly embarrassed about junking our previous plans. But when it came down to Miss Porter or Buddy there was no contest. Sports and caramel apples never could compete with the allure of sex. I knew Buddy would've done the same thing, but that didn't stop him from grumbling and calling me a "pansy."

When everyone had dispersed from the class, Miss Porter turned to me with that lulling gaze. "Why don't you fill the pail with water while I sort through this artwork, Zachary."

"Sure," I said. My heart was thumping so loudly I was afraid she'd hear it. So I closed my mouth tight to keep the beating quiet.

In the boy's washroom, I popped some Spearmint into my mouth, then checked my wave in the mirror, having forgotten I'd used almost half a jar of Brylcreem that morning. If I never washed my hair again, they could've buried me fifty years later with my pompadour still intact. I stood there looking at my reflection uneasily, waiting for the bucket to fill and my temperature to settle. When I finally wandered back inside my condition had become critical.

"We're glad you're b-back," I croaked. The plan was to keep my voice smooth like Bogey's. But I wasn't exactly in control of things.

"Thanks very much, Zachary. You certainly know how to make a girl feel good."

I tried not to blush or smile, but it was no use. I could feel my blood swell as a silly grin crept over my face. While I was gone, she'd piled her hair atop her head which made her look sexier than ever. Standing there, pail in hand, I suddenly became conscious of my breathing—sounding like our old refrigerator.

"You're spilling!" she pointed.

I reddened and stood frozen with my pail half-empty. There was a stain the size of New Jersey down my pants.

She grabbed a rag and bent over to sop up the mess. I watched her bend gracefully. "You know," she said, "I can't stop thinking about Mr. Bondi."

It took the words a good ten seconds to reach my brain as I was nearly hypnotized by the exposed nape of her neck. "Yeah, p-poor Mr. Bondi. Poor, poor Mr. Bondi."

Then she turned and looked up at me. When I realized I was stammering again, I started scrubbing the brushes furiously, confining my gaze to the soapy bucket. Anything to get my eyes off her. But my mind revolted, continuing to create sordid images in the suds as I pictured the two of us together in a bubble bath.

"I certainly hope those terrible lies and rumors about Mr. Bondi and our so-called romance stop," she said. "It's just not fair to his wife."

Lies? I thought. Those weren't lies. But then I realized Miss Porter probably thought *I* was the one who could help put an end to the rumors. Little did she know that Buddy and I knew that those rumors were fact.

"That's the trouble with small towns," she said. "Everyone's a gossip." As she placed a pile of artwork into the cabinet, she brushed close by me and I caught a whiff of that wonderful lilac perfume. I smiled dreamily, vacuuming up her wonderful scent. So what if she doesn't fess up, I thought. Nobody's perfect. Then she slipped back past me, but stopped suddenly and drew a long breath. Slowly, she turned around and cornered me with those hazel eyes. I could only stand there awkward, tongue-tied and grinning.

"You've got a real sweetness, Zachary. Your smile sort of reminds me of my brother."

"You've got a brother?"

"I used to."

I decided not to press it, so we passed the next few moments silently. But when we looked at each other, I made a conscious effort not to smile because I didn't want her reducing our affair into some lousy brother-sister relationship.

"I hope you're considering art school," she said, coming over to help me dry the brushes. "I have a feeling you'd do very well in a creative field. And there're some excellent schools in the area I'm sure you'd love."

Her hand grazed mine as we both reached for the same brush. Goosebumps claimed my flesh—and at that moment I knew too well what I'd "love," but it had nothing to do with art. "Actually, I want to play college ball," I said. "And I don't think an art school would be so hot for that. But I've also been thinking about something else . . ."

"And what's that?"

"Criminology."

She paused. "How fascinating."

"That's the science of criminal detection," I said, a little uncertainly. I'd picked up the word and definition from Roth.

"That's right," she remarked. "I'll bet you're the only one in class who knows what criminology means."

"Probably," I said, trying to sound modest.

"We could use policemen like you, Zachary. There's nothing more reassuring than an officer with a nice smile and a kind heart."

I quickly added "policeman" to my list of career possibilities.

∽✷

The *Waterbury Courier* reported that the top-ranking Nazis were all in custody, with the exception of Martin Bormann, Hitler's deputy and closest advisor in the final days. They were all set to be tried at Nuremberg for their crimes against humanity, much to the satisfaction of my folks.

My father angrily reacted to the sudden religious interest of the Nazis when the going got rough and how they started asking for Bibles as well as the services of U.S. Army chaplains. "Where the hell was their religious conviction when they massacred hundreds of thousands of our people?" he raged. Occasionally it was re-assuring to see my father vent his anger; it made me feel proud.

For my father, outbursts were rare. He usually kept things bottled up. But leave it to the Nazis to set him off. Ironically, I remember him once telling me with a grin that during the Battle of the Bulge, General Patton told a chaplain: "I want a prayer to stop the rain. If we get a few clear days, we could kill a couple hundred thousand krauts."

That afternoon the rain was pouring down. My

mother was off on business in Waterbury with our family lawyer and Lenny was rehearsing with the high school dance band. Lenny played sax and clarinet, and had been urging me to take trombone lessons. We both had worshipped Glenn Miller. In fact, the night Miller was reported missing in a military plane crash we sat dejected at the table and gave our favorite bandleader a full minute of silence before supper. My mother was mystified by the honor. "How come you didn't do anything like this for Uncle Ben when he passed away?" Lenny tried to explain that Uncle Ben couldn't play trombone, and besides, he wasn't even in the service.

With everybody gone, my father and I enjoyed the time alone. When we were together he would come alive. And he would always do his best to make me feel important, mentioning how lucky he was to have me as a son. "I just hope you tipped the stork," I'd say. And we'd both chuckle. I was just about the only one who could make my father laugh, with the possible exception of "The Edgar Bergen and Charlie McCarthy Show." My father was always delighted when Bergen would turn to Mortimer Snerd and ask: "Mortimer, how can you be so *stupid*?" To which Mortimer could only answer, "I'm not sure, Edgar."

"I hope you're taking Hebrew School seriously," my father said, out of the blue.

I was sitting at the soda fountain shoveling down spoonfuls of my father's ice cream specialty. It was the same concoction every time, but that was how I liked it, no surprises—one scoop of chocolate, one scoop of coffee and one vanilla smothered with Dolly chocolate syrup, chopped walnuts, whipped cream and three cherries. My mother, on the other hand, would always sneak in a spoonful of crushed fruit under the whipped cream "for vitamins."

"My bar mitzvah's four months away, Dad."

"Four months, that's right. But it's important you learn the meaning of Jewishness. I don't want you to just memorize the Torah and get nothing out of it."

"I thought I was *born* with the feeling of Jewishness." He didn't respond to that one. "Besides," I said, "I want to concentrate on sports this year. Football season's already half over."

"Football's half over, huh. Well, that's not such a terrible thing. I'd rather you play basketball anyway. Everybody gets hurt in football. It's so damn violent. What's the point? At least basketball takes a little skill."

That was the side of my father which used to annoy me most. He didn't know squat about sports. I couldn't help thinking that at least when Roth talked sports, he knew a thing or two.

10

The brisk New England weather began to settle in by late September. And mornings found the streets whitened with a thin layer of frost. Soon it would be Thanksgiving and we'd have our annual turkey dinner. Usually on the day after at school, the boasts would fly:

"We had a fifteen pounder!"

"Hell, we had at least a twenty-fiver!"

"I got sooo plastered on hard cider . . ."

"You should have seen how big *our* turkey was. Fed thirty plus two dogs and we still got enough left for sandwiches till New Year's."

Besides turkey, Thanksgiving was always a special holiday for the kids at Baldwin Grammar, probably because we were so close to Massachusetts and Plymouth Rock. School activities included cutting out jack-o-lanterns from large pumpkins and frying up the seeds, making muskets out of cardboard and dressing up to re-enact Colonial times. Unfortunately, everybody insisted on being Indians. No one wanted to be Pilgrims, with those dreary black costumes and ridiculous hats. Personally, I had a problem with those buckled shoes. I never could see myself in anything but Keds.

By the time Thanksgiving arrived, Smith's Pond and Black Rock were nearly frozen over, and only the boldest kids would venture out to test the ice.

"I don't want you skating till Christmas," my father announced annually. "It's not safe. There've been too many drownings over the years," he reasoned. But it was mostly the Canadians who were out there early. They had ice in their veins and didn't care if they fell through—this was surely part of the fun for them.

The Canucks, a splinter group of Oakville's lower class, lived south of Main Street in Oakville and mostly worked in the factories along with the few Slavics, Irish and Italians. Regardless of their social status, the Canadians had lots to brag about in 1945: Branch Rickey had just signed Negro athlete, Jackie Robinson, to play for the Brooklyn farm team in Montreal. I figured the Dodgers needed a postwar spark, whatever his color. And Maurice Richard was leading the Montreal Canadiens to yet another great hockey season. Toronto wasn't half-bad either.

On the north side of Main Street the class changed sharply. Almost everyone was Anglo and middle- to upper-class. Oakville High, Baldwin Grammar and Wentworth Prep were located on the north side. Buddy lived slightly south of Main, as did Miss Porter, who lived alone in a small saltbox. Heinz lived nearby with his ancient mother in one of the many shabby dwellings he'd somehow acquired in that part of town.

From the 30's until just recently, the railroad ran parallel to the river and transported products to the bigger cities near the Long Island Sound and New York. But during the war, it was unusual to see a train. Maibaum said they needed all the steel for tanks and that trains were too easy a target for bombers. Oakville Textile and Keller Plastic were south, as were Smith's Pond and the railway tracks. The Kellers actually lived across from Wentworth Prep on the north side. By the early 40's, though, Wentworth himself had little family or fortune left to speak of, making the Kellers Oakville's wealthiest residents.

Saul Keller, a former Berlin industrialist, had managed to escape Hitler, and he forever let everyone know how dearly he paid to accomplish that. Keller always looked out of place around Oakville in his Continental-cut tweeds and thick horn-rims. On a typical stroll down Main Street he'd receive lots of polite nods, but never one genuine "Hi, how're you, Saul?" The Kellers had two kids: Stephen, fifteen, who attended Wentworth, the local WASP prep school, and Candy, thirteen, who went to some fancy girls' school in upstate New York.

Politically, Oakville was annoyingly simple and corrupt. Mayor Avery Wentworth's family, which went back to Colonial times, were founders of the prep school and had been running local government with an iron hand for years. My father liked to point out that "Germany wasn't the only fascist state in the world." But almost everyone else in town was disillusioned, too. Because of the war though, the problem of Wentworth seemed minuscule.

Following the war, Truman set the tone for reform: "It's time for Americans to cut out the foolishness and get back to work." The whole country seemed to develop a strong sense of ethics, and Oakville was no exception. The town council called for a special off-year election, creating an exciting buzz in the air.

Unfortunately, our leading mayoral candidate was in the slammer. Pat Ryan had run on a strong platform to rid Oakville of its old guard, primarily Big Lew. And Ryan, with connections in Hartford, brought a sense of the outside world to Oakville. Clearly the popular choice, he promised to help convert the factories back to peacetime production and resume full employment. If the election had been held before school started, Ryan's victory would have been a landslide. But with the town's favorite son behind bars, we were left with only Wentworth and his strongman, Heinz.

It was no secret that Avery Wentworth had Big Lew in his back pocket or vice versa, no one was really sure which. Nevertheless, a few days after the murder, I spotted Heinz swaggering along Main Street tearing down "Ryan for Mayor" posters from the telephone poles. It was then that I first wondered how far Big Lew would actually go to keep Oakville just the way it was.

❧

The seventh and eighth graders were excused from morning classes to attend Mr. Bondi's memorial ceremony at Oakwood Fields. It was always a blessing to get excused from classes, but this instance was tainted as someone had to die for the privilege. So we all walked in a silent, single-file line from school, across town to the cemetery.

In addition to Bondi's immediate family and colleagues, a number of his buddies from the Air Force attended. Miss Porter, glamorously veiled in black, watched alone from a distance under a gnarled elm tree. It was hard to tell if she was crying, but I distinctly remember how scared and lonely she looked standing there and clutching herself. I wanted to go offer my arm for support. After our last talk, I felt like I was her only friend. No matter how involved she was in the murder, I couldn't help feeling sorry for her.

Standing only about twenty feet from the preacher, I was strangely unconscious of his eulogy. My attention was fixed on Bondi's wife, Cora, who looked pathetically sallow as she scattered her husband's remains to the winds. That morning, I'd learned from my mother that she was Ryan's kid sister, which definitely shed a new light on things. I could only assume that when Ryan caught Bondi cheating on Cora, he went berserk, being exactly the kind of guy to look out for his little sister no matter what the consequence. I studied Cora intently and wondered if she had any inkling about her husband's involvement with Miss Porter. There was no doubt she had heard the rumors.

Lieutenant Roth, in classic detective style, was observing the scene from his spot behind the preacher. Earlier, I'd told him my theory about the Heinz-Wentworth conspiracy, but he didn't seem interested. "This is bigger than small town politics," Roth said. "Much bigger."

As the preacher waxed on, Buddy leaned close to me and whispered, "So where's Big Lew?"

"I sure as hell didn't invite him."

"If he had any brains," Buddy said, "he'd be here." Then he smiled smugly. "It would have been the perfect sham."

Just as he said that, I spotted something across the grass. Parked in the shadows about fifty feet away was the patrol car. With his cap off in reverence, Heinz watched the service from a distance.

"I hope this doesn't mean Big Lew's actually got brains," I whispered. Buddy couldn't even muster a response as his mouth flopped open in awe.

Tugging on the lieutenant's sleeve, I indicated Heinz with my head. But Roth only grinned, like it was all part of his plan. I had nothing to grin about though, as I could sense Big Lew glaring at me across the tombstones. There was malice in his eyes—more than usual it seemed—and it dawned on me that he probably knew I'd witnessed the killing but was just waiting for the perfect time to put *me* six feet under.

By the time the service ended, the clouds had darkened and a cold wind whisked across the fields, dropping the temperature. As Heinz drove away, Roth said he had to take off too and left Buddy and me to pay our last respects. I didn't enjoy the prospect of walking home unprotected, but I figured I had no choice.

Buddy and I stared down at Bondi's gravestone until a relentless gust chilled us to the bones. "It's so damn cold," Buddy said, "my nose won't even run. Must be frozen over."

Heading back, we cut through the woods towards the main roadway back to town. The sound of workers ripping nails and shattering glass echoed as we passed the site of the old Spotting Tower, which was presently being dismantled.

"I can't believe they're tearing that down."

Though it symbolized the end of the war, we couldn't help but be saddened. "Suppose there's another war," Buddy said. "Then they gotta build a whole new one."

"There's not gonna be another war. You think they're stupid?"

In 1943 Buddy and I offered to help patrol the skies at the Spotting Tower in search of enemy planes. We were provided with official charts depicting silhouettes of every enemy aircraft—German and Japanese—binoculars, CD armbands and a special security phone number that I still recall: Army Flash, 1228.

The Civil Defense Department had presented us each with plaques, inscribed: "To the youngest volunteer ever allowed on the tower, you are an inspiration and proud symbol of America's youth." It more than fulfilled our wildest fantasies. And despite all the deaths and atrocities of World War II, we used to compare the excitement to the seventh game of the 1940 World Series, when, as Buddy put it, "Cincy creamed those A.L. chump Tigers." It was no wonder we found it hard to buy the saying: "War is Hell."

11

The course in school I liked best was art, but Miss Porter wasn't the only reason. Art had no homework, no tests, and no boring lectures. Mostly, though, it was the release I got from drawing. Besides sports, my energy needed someplace to go and art filled the bill. At twelve, my only true talent was copying cartoon strip characters, but according to Miss Porter I definitely had artistic potential. "You're a real artist," she said, "not afraid to draw what you feel. And that's more important than skill." Needless to say, I devoured the praise like a fistful of fudge.

Miss Porter taught both art and music at Baldwin Grammar as well as Oakville High—she zipped between the two schools in her beat-up Ford, juggling classes. Luckily, she didn't drive like the other women in Oakville. She'd smoothly accelerate into turns and generally disregard the speed limit—not recklessly, but smoothly, I remember. That was just another item on the endless list of things I admired about her.

In my heart, I wanted to pursue art as a career—not just to please Miss Porter, but because I fancied the idea of drawing for money. I had trouble with the image of an artist, though. I couldn't relinquish my dreams of Joe DiMaggio, Glenn Davis and Doc Blanchard—visions of national heroes with millions of fans. Art was a great hobby, I thought, but as a career it seemed lonely and lacking in glory. Artists seemed like frail, pipe-smoking guys who lived alone with their work; an impression I gleaned from radio dramas. And as a kid, it was much more fun to imagine myself in Ebbets Field making a perfect throw home to win the Series or better yet, sinking the winning hoop for N.Y.U. at Madison Square Garden.

Nevertheless, my attraction to Miss Porter grew and I soon found myself staying after school to help her. Buddy was convinced I was just buttering her up for an "A."

"I could get an 'A' in art with my eyes closed," I said.

Buddy scoffed at the notion. But we both knew that if I actually managed to land Miss Porter it would be the single greatest feat in Oakville's history. And although Buddy claimed I was just wasting my time, those afternoons with Miss Porter were like trips to heaven for me. All my senses came alive, and at night, lying in bed, I would vividly recall every detail of our time together.

One day, when Miss Porter asked me to show her an example of work by my favorite artist, I brought in a cover from the *Saturday Evening Post* illustrated by Norman Rockwell. I'd always admired Rockwell's work—often trying in vain to recreate *Post* covers. But rather than becoming discouraged, I gained an even greater respect for Rockwell's talent. That particular illustration depicted a young G.I. being welcomed home by his family and friends. In the left-hand corner of the picture, a bobbysoxer, who reminded me of Melissa, hid shyly behind a tree. Obviously she was in love with the young soldier.

"I saw this when it came out," Miss Porter said. "It's wonderful." I was glad she liked it too. "The boy in the picture kind of resembles you with those big brown eyes."

I could feel myself blushing.

"No one captures America like Rockwell," she said.

"You said it. He's terrific."

"I've told you this before, Zachary," she said, "but I think you have an unusual art talent. And with decent training, I truly believe you can go places. Maybe even be the next Rockwell."

I could feel the blood rush to my ears.

"I suspect you have a similar musical gift," she added. "Music and art go hand-in-hand, you know."

"Actually, my brother . . . he plays sax and clarinet, and he thinks I should take up the trombone." The truth was, I'd tried Lenny's saxophone a couple of times only to discover that in my case, music and art most certainly did not go hand-in-hand.

"Why *not* the trombone?" she said. "I can't teach it, but that sounds like a great idea."

"Well," I said, "if I was going to learn music, I'd rather learn something *you* can teach." I felt like I'd just laid my cards on the table with a thousand bucks in the pot.

After a few moments she said, "How do you feel about the cello?"

"Huh?" Visions of Eddie "The Violin" and his lousy batting average filled my head.

"Cello," she repeated. "Now *that* I could teach."

"I don't know . . ." I just couldn't picture Rocky

Graziano or any great athlete, for that matter, playing a stringed instrument.

In a blatant effort to sway my impressionable mind, she removed a cello from a large black case leaning against her desk. I could feel my ears warm as she gently positioned the instrument between her spread legs and began playing. Maybe the cello wasn't such a bad idea, I thought. In fact, I wished I was a cello at that very moment.

She played beautifully; her eyes closed, her head swaying gracefully to the luscious melody. I was on cloud nine and soaring. Not only was the music heavenly, but watching Miss Porter clasp the cello with such unbridled passion excited my every cell. I stared, entranced, as her fingers moved delicately over the strings. Then a thought struck me like a sour note: those lovely hands actually touching Big Lew!

When she finished playing we sat together silently, until I finally worked up my nerve. "Would you mind if I say something personal?"

"Depends," she said, smiling innocently.

"I just don't know what you see in Officer Heinz."

I imagined she was attracted to her opposite— something like my mother and father. No doubt she liked her men rough and tumble, I thought. And Big Lew was as rough as they came in Oakville. After an awkward pause, she started to put the cello away. Obviously, she didn't want to discuss it.

"Sorry," I said. "It's probably none of my business."

"That's okay," she smiled. "I'm sure you're not the only one who's wondered about us." I waited for her to continue. "Why don't you help me out to the

car with this stuff," she said, indicating a large port-
folio and briefcase.

The topic seemed closed. It was four o'clock and
all the corridors were empty as we walked down the
hallway, our footsteps echoing.

"Let's put it this way," she added, "it's not what
you think."

For her to admit their relationship wasn't what I
thought was a positive sign. If she really cared for
Heinz, I reasoned, she would have told me. As we
approached the side exit which led to the parking lot,
I started to open the door. And I wasn't surprised to
spot Big Lew outside through the glass, sitting in the
Olds coupe, waiting.

༈

I wandered home taking the slow route through
town rather than the back way along the river bank
and through the cemetery. I struggled with my first
career decision: art or sports? Before I could decide,
though, Roth's Packard pulled up alongside me. The
passenger door eased open, beckoning. I would have
preferred to continue walking alone, but I knew the
lieutenant wanted something.

We exchanged brief greetings then took off on one
of our customary spins where he drove us out to the
edge of town then turned around at Gino's and
headed back. For a change, Roth didn't grill me. I
could tell he was troubled.

"Big Lew was waiting for Miss Porter in that same

Olds coupe Buddy and I saw him getting into at the hospital."

"Oh?"

"Yeah, but he wasn't driving that time and we couldn't make out who was. Buddy thought it looked like Wentworth. But I don't know."

"I'm sure Miss Porter would know," Roth said.

I straightened up. "Well, I can find out 'cause she kinda likes me. I'm her favorite student."

Roth smiled. "I'll bet you are." It was getting dark outside. "We should keep in constant touch, Zachary," Roth said. "In order for my plan to work, I need to know every move that Heinz and Miss Porter make. So let's say that'll be your beat. Heinz and Miss Porter. Got it?"

"What do you mean, 'my beat'?"

"Your beat is your assignment. I'm assigning you to Heinz and Miss Porter. From a distance," he added. "*Just observe.*"

I was thrilled about having my own "beat," and as we cruised down Main Street, I hoped that all my classmates would notice us, especially Buddy.

"Only thing I need now," I said, trying to sound like Cagney, "is a .38 like yours."

Roth swerved the car over to the curb near the apartment, slammed on the brakes and glared at me. "Don't think this is a game, because it isn't! This is serious business." I swallowed nervously. "You can be a great help to me, Zachary. But the moment you start fooling around, it'll be the end of it. So when I say I want you to *just observe,* I mean it." He thumped the steering wheel nervously. "I want Heinz, but I don't want you getting hurt, Zack. It's as simple as that." There was a pause, and I took a deep breath.

"Good night," Roth said.

I opened the car door, thinking I'd walk the rest of the way. "Good night." As "The Pack" pulled away I decided to run.

12

Next morning I was still stinging from Roth's repri-
mand, but more determined than ever to hold my
own. I may not carry a badge or a gun, I reasoned, but
at least I had a lot of good questions. And that seemed
the perfect cover as everyone would think it was just
my "kid curiosity."

I found Maibaum in the kitchen right where I expected, hunched over breakfast with that don't-
bother-me look. Not wasting time with chitchat, I
started my first interrogation.

"Hey Dave, ever notice anyone at the factory driving an Olds coupe?"

Maibaum barely regarded me as he spread a gob of
marmalade over his toast. "I'm too busy to spot stuff
like that," he said, folding the bread to fit his mouth.
"Keller's on my back from the moment I punch in."
He finished his food with a final swig of coffee, then
picked up and left for work.

Detective work is tough, I thought, nobody ever
tells you what you want to hear. Although, it
should've crossed my mind that being a kid might
have had something to do with it.

By the time I'd scavenged together a breakfast,
Lenny appeared in his shorts, looking bedraggled.
"Mornin' kid," he muttered, as he plucked the last
piece of bacon from my plate. Lenny's hair was rag-
ged and the little growth of beard on his face looked

like grime. Hoisting a bottle of milk from the fridge, he eyed the top's missing contents. "I see 'The Baum' has already struck."

Lenny did have a unique sense of humor, and I loved it when he called Dave "The Baum." Lenny just ambled through life without worrying much about anything. His job at Elmer's Alleys always seemed to keep him loaded with pocket money, which I truly envied. Unfortunately, my father didn't allow me to set up pins. The one time Lenny let me try, some joker bowled a ball before I was able to climb out of the pit. The pins went flying, and so did I. Luckily, I didn't suffer any serious damage, but all hopes for a career as a pinsetter came to an abrupt end when the manager called my parents.

As much as Lenny's carefree lifestyle was to be admired, you had to seriously question his future. There was the dental school angle, but I always suspected even our parents knew that was hogwash. It was painfully clear that Lenny had no intention of going to college. He enjoyed simply taking things as they came. "There's always gonna be air to breathe and water to drink," he philosophized. "Things have a way of working out."

"Lenny's got a lot to say," my father remarked. "But so do parrots. Don't take everything that comes out of your brother's mouth seriously and you'll do fine." At about that point I realized it wasn't right for a younger brother to worry about an older brother.

"Now that the war's over," Lenny announced, "I think I'll enlist." I just shook my head as he leaned against the stove and took a long gulp of milk straight from the bottle. "I'll be eligible for the G.I. Bill," he continued. "But I won't have to go fight any damn war and lose any chunks of my hide."

"What about dental school?"

"The Army's gonna make me rich, kid."

Picturing Lenny rising and shining every morning in some army barracks was unthinkable. Joining the military was against everything he stood for: discipline, commitment, and responsibility. The only part that made sense to me was the pride he seemed to take in beating the system.

When I started to leave, Lenny hooked me by the arm. "Hope yer not in any trouble, kid. You got that guilty look." He knew as well as anyone that if Big Lew was asking questions about me, I must be hiding something. But I kept mum.

"Just keep lookin' over your shoulder, bub. 'Cause they don't play fair, ya know." I had no idea who "they" were, but I absorbed the message anyway. It was Lenny's way of saying he cared about me.

Hurrying out the door and down the steps, I was hoping to catch Melissa before Latin class. I'd been banking on copying her homework—a habit I was becoming addicted to. Concentrating during classes was becoming increasingly difficult also, not that it was something which ever came naturally. The murder was occupying most of my thoughts, and until Heinz was behind bars nothing else mattered.

Peering around the classroom I watched as—two desks in front of me and on the right—Melissa properly recited what we'd been assigned to read, then proceeded to answer several questions with perfect ease. Sitting behind her was nice. It allowed me to study her pretty hair and body positions undetected.

Mr. Murphy, the new, young history teacher who had taken over for Bondi, was at the blackboard monotonously listing reasons for the feudal breakdown. As he noted the chivalrous aspects of the Renaissance, I considered the notion of fighting to the death for a woman. Soon I found myself doodling a sketch of Miss Porter with myself at the altar. Buddy, looking goofy as ever, was my best man. "Zachary and Mary Beth Silver" I scrolled in fancy letters across the top of the drawing. Now there's someone I'd fight for—my own Helen of Troy.

"Would you like to add anything to these observations, Zachary?" Murphy asked, rudely interrupting my daydream.

I am convinced Murphy could tell who of his students were prepared and who were not, and he took special pleasure in making an example of the "nots."

"No thanks," I said, embarrassed.

There were a few snickers.

I hated being caught by surprise. Lenny was right; they don't play fair.

13

I can still remember the day Buddy came up with his solution to the problem of time. "We need eight days a week so you can have one day with me." It wasn't a bad idea, what with the impossible schedule I was juggling; the case, schoolwork and sports, not to mention my newfound love-life. And with winter approaching, it was getting dark earlier. Time was definitely not on my side, and so when what precious few hours of daylight I had were squandered, I became understandably unraveled.

Since I attended Hebrew school in Waterbury, and my mother was meeting there with our family lawyer, she had arranged to pick me up at 4:30. By 4:50 I started getting antsy at the thought of missing out on basketball with Buddy again.

Despite her frequent delays, I actually preferred riding home with my mother, even though the trip took twenty minutes longer than the bus. Lenny had already soured me on public transportation by telling me about some kid in Naugatuck who'd taken the wrong bus and ended up in Philadelphia without enough money to call his parents. "For all I know," Lenny said, "the rug rat was picked up and strangled." So when I finally spotted my mother chugging up the avenue in our '39 gray Buick which Lenny had dubbed the "Silvermobile," I was relieved to say the least.

The "Silvermobile" was a testament to the endurance of Detroit manufacturing. Aside from a few minor dents in the body, the engine still churned as heartily as the day we bought it. My mother had been advised several times by our lawyer that it was time to trade the ol' war horse in for a new one. This excited Lenny and me to no end; especially Lenny as he was nearly ready to drive himself. But my mother reasoned that until we could afford the latest model, she would continue to drive the Buick slow and steady like a Sherman tank in an effort to conserve what little life it had left. And since she did all the driving in the family—my father simply decided to quit one day, claiming there was already enough stress in his life—my mother had final say in the matter.

Her biggest problem behind the wheel was that she couldn't steer and talk at the same time. This meant conversations took place only at full stops and traffic lights.

"Sorry I'm late," she said, pulling up to the curb. She was disheveled and flustered as usual. Meetings with our lawyer seemed to do that to her. As she maneuvered the Buick carefully and silently through traffic, nothing else was uttered.

Dusk cast long shadows across the road as we made our way home and I stared out at the Colonial-style houses set back from the street; there were about four on each block, with room for eight. How many times I envied the spacious gardens, imagining myself romping with a puppy on the rolling lawns.

We passed the large Catholic Church with its elegant elms, located between Oakville and Waterbury. I had asked my father once to take me to Mass there, just to satisfy my curiosity. But he declined, insisting that I wasn't old enough to "take that stuff with a grain of salt." For years afterward my image of a Catholic service was something straight out of one of those Lon Chaney horror films.

"I really believed things would be easier now," my mother blurted as she slowed for a light, "But stupid me, nothing's changed."

"What do you mean?" I asked, still gazing out the car window.

"Now don't go and tell your father I mentioned anything," she said, "but ever since the war, Officer Heinz has been extorting money from us. And our lawyer just informed me we may not have enough money to send Leonard to dental school."

"What's extorting?"

"We have to pay that crooked cop twenty dollars a week as protection money."

The light turned green and we proceeded.

"Protection from what?"

Of course, she couldn't reply until we made it to the next light.

I repeated the question: "Protection from what, Mom?"

"Supposedly Heinz protects us from the town's anti-Semites."

I knew that word well. It was one of my father's favorites. "But he's the biggest one of all," I said. "Besides, the war's over."

"Well, he's still making us pay. Only now he wants

thirty dollars because he says times are hard since he's been suspended.''

She tried to remain calm, but I could hear the frustration in her voice. "I just wish your father would tell Heinz to go to hell.''

That I could never imagine.

We drove along silently until the next stoplight. "Heinz has been doing the same thing with the Kellers, you know. Only worse,'' she added. "Saul's paying out two hundred a week.''

Sure enough, as we hit Main Street it was dark and I realized I'd have to forget basketball with Buddy. It was for the best, though, because when I was angry, my setshot was off, and as we pulled up in front of Silver's General, I had worked myself into a silent fury at the idea of Big Lew extorting money from our family.

Business hours at our store were 9 A.M. to 9 P.M. For lunch and dinner, either my father or mother would take over downstairs, while the other came upstairs for a meal. I usually had dinner with my father, Lenny with my mother. My father and I always enjoyed cooking together, especially while listening to the kitchen radio. Every day at 5:30 when "Jack Armstrong, the All-American Boy'' would come on, we would sing along together with the show's theme song, which is permanently etched in my brain:

"Have you tried Wheaties?
They're whole wheat with all of the bran.
Won't you try Wheaties?
For wheat is the best food of man!
They're crispy and crunchy the whole
year through.
Jack Armstrong never tires of them
And neither will you.
So just buy Wheaties
The best breakfast food in the land!"

By sending in various box tops and the appropriate coinage, anyone could receive doodads like a Jack Armstrong Pedometer, Tom Mix Ranger Knife, Secret Norden Bombsight or Whistling Ring—all of which I owned and cherished. But only kids like me who were involved in a real police case would find them handy I reasoned.

My favorite gadget was the Pedometer: "Just hang your Pedometer on belt or pocket, and hike. It'll keep track of every step you take. Lots of fun to watch. Counts every step. Have your pals guess how far it is to camping grounds. Prove with Pedometer who's nearest right!" Of course I had no intention of determining how far it was to a campsite—mainly because we never went camping, but also because I believed my Pedometer would be used for infinitely more important endeavors.

By the time I washed up for dinner, Jack Armstrong had already deserted the airwaves and my father was tuned into yet another newscast and commentary by Gabriel Heatter. When Heatter had interesting stories, I sort of enjoyed listening too. The best one we ever heard together was when Heatter informed us that President Truman, once a haberdasher, had also been a storekeeper. Heatter then proceeded to tell how Truman had dropped into a Men's Wear Shop owned by his ex-partner in Kansas City, looked over the stock, then bought eighteen pairs of size eleven socks.

My father and I grinned as the newscaster continued: "Then Harry went to his old barbershop."

Heatter liked playing all the parts:

"Usual trim, Harry?"

"None of the fancy stuff now. I don't want anything that smells."

Everybody loved Truman back then, except of course, the Japanese, who weren't too keen on what had happened at Hiroshima and Nagasaki. But those were not the kinds of problems that usually concerned me—they were too distant and too broad. It was impossible to feel the repercussions of something like the A-Bomb in Oakville, especially when you had Big Lew to worry about.

14

Roth's Packard was waiting across the street when I left the apartment after breakfast. I knew the lieutenant was inside the car as the windows were all fogged up. Looking around to make sure my father wasn't watching, I darted for the passenger door—knowing full well that being seen hopping into a strange vehicle would get his pressure up.

Roth, wearing a tan topcoat and leather gloves, greeted me with a nod and offered me a bite of the Danish he was nibbling.

"No thanks." As a kid I had a peeve about sharing food. "Did you know Heinz has been extorting money from my family," I announced right off the bat.

Roth glanced at me coolly. "I know all about that. Your family and the Kellers primarily. But he's been on the take from other families in town too."

I was constantly amazed at how much Roth actually knew. "Can't we nail him now, then?"

"You've gotta learn to be patient, Zack. Ninety percent of policework is patience."

I sighed. All I could think of was that Heinz was a cold-blooded killer and I wanted him convicted and out of action—fast.

"Look at it this way. You're at the top of the key and, sure you could go ahead and take the shot, but you'd be better off waiting for someone to make a nice cut then slip him a great pass."

I appreciated the basketball analogy, but had a hard time with the "patience" nonetheless. Besides, the last thing I wanted was a lecture before school. I got my fill of that five days a week. "It's hard to be patient when I'm probably next on Big Lew's hit list."

"What makes you say that?"

I hesitated, sorry I'd blabbed. "I don't know," I shrugged; this, of course, being the response-of-choice among kids with something to hide.

"Don't worry, I'll keep an eye on you. I promise." He patted me on the shoulder for reassurance. "I've got a date with Bondi's widow this afternoon," Roth said. "How'd you like to come along?"

"Date?"

"An appointment to speak with her," he said. "Maybe you can help me out." Noticing my perked expression, he quickly added: "After school."

I felt like a kid being offered candy. "What are we gonna talk to her about?"

"Ever since the murder she hasn't spoken with Ryan," Roth reported. "I just want to feel out the situation, see what she knows."

"Maybe she thinks Coach did it," I eagerly suggested.

"Could be," Roth mumbled, lost in thought. "Hey, I'd better get you to class," he said suddenly. "I've got to see Ryan now."

"I'll bet *he's* having trouble being patient."

"Actually," Roth said, "Coach Ryan is being a good sport, considering."

Roth dropped me off at the far end of the school parking lot. I didn't realize it at the time, but my life changed that afternoon when the lieutenant unofficially made me his partner.

∽✗

Buddy and I separated after school, planning to meet later to gather players for a scrub game of touch football. It seemed like we were always the ones rounding up kids for pickup games. And I often wondered if we shouldn't have charged some sort of "organizational fee" for our efforts.

Heading towards the police station to meet Roth, I sensed something wrong. I stopped and checked both directions. The streets and sidewalks were empty. The sun was already setting and shadows stretched across the avenue. A familiar knot of fear tightened in my belly.

Throughout my early school years, Carl Judd, the class bully, regularly threatened to beat me up. And during basketball, especially if I scored on him, Judd would taunt me with "Lucky Jeeewwboy!" Because he out-weighed and towered over me, I never had the guts to tell him it wasn't luck, but rather superior skill. For a stretch of time near the beginning of fifth grade, nearly every day I was forced to hightail it home right after the school bell to avoid being caught and soundly thumped by Judd. Luckily, the one time he did catch me, some grown-ups were around, so he let me off with a few curses and a couple of hard kicks. By sixth grade, I had grown two inches taller and came to realize Judd was nothing more than hot air—at which time he redirected his vengeance upon a short Italian kid he called the "Little Wopper."

I don't know exactly what made me stop on the street corner that day. My legs locked and all movement was arrested. Then my fear took shape as Big Lew emerged from an alley and squared up, waiting for me. Although he was grinning, I was certain he had anything but a friendly visit in mind.

"We should talk, Silver," he growled.

Not in the mood for idle chatter, I managed to coax my legs into motion and proceeded to angle across the street. Once on the other side, I paused to look around. Sure enough, Big Lew was right on my tail, striding towards me with what seemed like deadly determination. That sickening sensation of mortal fear, like when Judd was at my heels, seized my frantic body. My pulse quickened and my breath grew short. Picking up my pace and racing along Elm Street, I caught a glimpse of Roth's Packard passing by up ahead.

Thinking I could cut him off at the corner of Main and First, I turned down an alley and sprinted for my life. But Big Lew was right on my ass. Bursting onto Main Street, I charged in front of "The Pack," which screeched to a stop in my path and nearly flattened me. I looked up at the sky thankfully, then piled into the front seat and tried to regain my breath.

"What the hell's going on?" Roth demanded.

I proceeded to tell him about Big Lew chasing me. But the lieutenant didn't appear to take me seriously.

"You sure it was Heinz?"

"Look at my hands." They were still shaking.

"Maybe he just wanted to talk."

"Talk about what, where he's gonna bury me if I keep helping you?"

"If you don't know anything, you've got nothing to be scared of, right?"

I felt like a "sittin' duck waitin' for the stew"—an expression I'd picked up from Lenny. But I just couldn't bring myself to confess. So I shrugged, as if Roth had raised a good point. We remained quiet for a while, driving across town at a pace I knew my mother would have approved of. "Where're we going?" I finally asked.

"How soon we forget. To the Bondi house. And when we get there, *I'll* do the talking. If you want to chime in, just give me a look like this first." He turned to me and arched his eyebrows. "Got it?"

I agreed, practicing with my eyebrows in the windscreen reflection the whole way there.

Bondi had lived in the same paint-peeling saltbox with his wife, Cora, since their marriage shortly after the start of the war. I don't remember the wedding, but my mother knew all about it. Apparently, years earlier, old Mrs. Ryan had been a regular customer at our store. And no social event in Oakville, however big or small, ever escaped my mother.

"My mother says that Cora and Pat Ryan are really close as brother and sister."

Roth remained silent, evidently mulling things over as we drove south below Main Street.

"Hey I just thought of something," I said. "What's Mrs. Bondi gonna think I'm doing with you?"

"I'll tell her the truth, that you're helping me out because you're so familiar with the town. I'm from Waterbury, remember? I need a guide."

It sounded reasonable enough, but I worried about my status on the case. In my mind there was a distinct difference between "partner" and "guide."

We finally pulled up to a small, gray house with a shabby garden and gnarled apple tree in front. Fall had come and gone and the start of winter was giving the trees a stark look. Nothing was green anymore. The days were shorter and it felt cold now. As I climbed out of the Packard, I watched a couple of fifth graders tossing a pigskin around in the street and it hit me. All of a sudden, without warning, I experienced a tremendous sense of loss. I can't explain it, but somehow I realized right at that moment that there weren't going to be too many more summers left to enjoy swimming at Black Rock with Buddy, talking about the pennant race and girls over a couple of smokes.

Buddy was right; we needed that eighth day.

15

While waiting for Cora to answer the front door, Roth reminded me that he was going to do all the talking. I nodded, and arched my eyebrows again. Roth smirked. When the door opened, Cora Bondi greeted us with a forced smile, hardly acknowledging my presence.

"Would you like coffee?" she asked. "And how 'bout some milk and cookies, Zachary?"

I almost broke my vow of silence and said yes, but quickly caught myself and nodded. Roth frowned. After she disappeared into the kitchen, Roth checked out the room and studied the wall portrait of Bondi in dress uniform. On the fireplace mantel were Greg's service medals and a hand-painted model of a B-17, the plane he'd piloted.

Cora returned with a tray containing two cups of coffee, a glass of milk and chocolate chip cookies, which looked homemade. A sucker for anything with chocolate, I grabbed a handful. Roth glared at me.

"We were very close, Pat and I," she said. "Until the killing."

Roth sipped his coffee and skillfully eased her into rambling. I was impressed; he was quite the smoothie.

Cora moved to the portrait, then turned to Roth, her eyes misty. "Did you know my husband was shot down in an air strike over Cologne?" She didn't wait for a response. "Lucky for all of us, Greg survived.

He was captured, then imprisoned. But he came home and said *I* was the one who kept him going over there. You know how good that made me feel?"

Roth nodded. I followed his lead. But no one was paying attention to me. As the tears began streaming down her face, I looked away. I'd heard it all before anyway—the Captain Bondi story had been well-publicized. Even *Look* had done an article.

"Greg told me how cruel the Germans were, treating the POW's like animals. The food was infested with vermin, and disease killed most everyone who lived through the torture." She bit her lip to hold back the tears. "We never treated *our* prisoners like that. Did we, Lieutenant?"

"No," Roth said sympathetically.

I filched another cookie.

Then, Roth proceeded: "Coach Ryan tells me you might know something about a Nazi officer, Mrs. Bondi?"

This was news to me.

Cora regained her composure. "Yes. Greg told me there was one S.S. Officer he'd never forget," she said. "He was the one who gave the order for Greg to be tortured after they captured him." She took a deep breath. "They made him strip down and lie naked on the cold floor for twelve hours while they questioned him. And Greg said he had to actually stay there and wet himself because they wouldn't let him up. Can you believe that?" She dabbed her eyes with a hanky. "Thank God he escaped before they killed him. I know they would've, too." She reached over and touched the Purple Heart displayed on the mantel. "Greg was an American hero," she said. "And there wasn't a person in the United States who didn't love him."

"I know," Roth said. "So what happened when Greg returned home?" he continued.

She sipped her coffee. "Well, he'd been honorably discharged, you know. And everything was going just fine, until last summer when Greg stopped in for pie at May's Diner one afternoon." She paused, trying to recall the details. "Just as he was paying his check, Greg spotted that very S.S. Officer who'd made him lie in his own . . ."

"May's Diner on Elm?" I interrupted, astounded. Arched eyebrows be damned, I wanted an answer.

Cora looked at me directly for the first time. Roth sighed.

"Yes." She returned her gaze to Roth. "Greg said they just stood there, frozen, staring at each other for what seemed like a whole minute. Greg wanted to say something. But he couldn't. He was speechless."

"Then what?" Roth asked.

"Then the man slipped out the door and disappeared," she said. "Greg was absolutely stunned."

"He didn't say *anything*?" I asked, unable to contain my curiosity. My eyes darted to Roth, who had all but given up on me.

Now Cora addressed me directly, shaking her head. "Well, Greg let a couple days go by, but he couldn't sleep. He just lay in bed all night, sometimes even crying. I guess he thought I was asleep. But I couldn't sleep either. I'd never seen him cry before."

I lowered my eyes; the idea of Bondi weeping disturbed me deeply.

"Finally, I talked Greg into telling the authorities there was a Nazi here. So he went to Lew Heinz and told him he could positively identify a man in town as a Nazi Officer."

"And what exactly did Heinz do?" Roth asked.

"He told Greg that was *impossible* and to forget the whole thing. He even went as far as to suggest Greg see a head doctor. But that just made Greg furious. He got so upset he couldn't eat, let alone sleep. Greg must've lost ten pounds in a week. He looked so gaunt and tired." She sighed hopelessly. "I tried to talk with him about it."

"Is that when he told Coach Ryan?" Roth asked.

"That's right," she said. "Greg never trusted Heinz anyway. And you can imagine how Pat feels about Big Lew." I nodded, and she continued. "Apparently, Pat confronted Heinz about it and threatened to call the F.B.I. if the matter was ignored. That's just the way Pat is. Real brash and fiery." Then, she turned to Roth and tried to speak calmly. "Seems to me that if anyone was going to be killed, it would've been Pat, not Greg."

❧

"That came off pretty good," Roth remarked as we drove away from the Bondi house.

"Did I talk too much?"

"You were fine," he said. "I think we're going to make a helluva team."

I was pleased, but something was nagging me. "Why didn't you tell me about the Nazi?"

"I wanted to see your reaction," Roth explained. "I'm still curious as to how much you know, Zachary."

Looking out the side window, I decided not to respond.

I liked working with Roth. He knew all the slick detective tricks. Now relaxed, he lit up a Muriel and took slow satisfied puffs. I was still confused about the Nazi angle, but confident Roth had a handle on that aspect—which was all that mattered since he was the one with the master plan. As I checked my watch, Roth glanced over at me and grinned.

"How were the cookies?"

"Not bad." It was already five to six, and unfortunately, I'd already missed "Jack Armstrong." But Bill Stern, probably the best sportscaster around, was just about to start his program. So I asked if we could tune him in on the car radio. Clamping the cigar in his teeth, Roth twiddled the knobs. After a few moments of getting nothing but fuzz, he gave up.

"Must be the weather," he said, giving it a final try. "This thing usually brings in every station from New York to Philadelphia."

"So who do you think has the best team in college basketball?" I asked, determined to prove I knew more about sports than he did.

"Oklahoma A & M," Roth answered without missing a beat.

I was surprised he knew that. "And who's your favorite boxer?"

"Willie Pep," he said, just as quickly.

I liked Pep, too. He was a scrappy featherweight

who fought out of Hartford. And as hardly anyone famous in sports came from The Nutmeg State, I was a big Pep fan.

"You know, he hails from Connecticut," Roth added.

I rolled my eyes. "Everybody and their mother knows that." I didn't mind that he was way ahead of me with detective stuff, that was understandable. But I wanted to be the sports maven.

"Tell you what," Roth said, stopping to let me off. "If and when we wrap up this case, I'll take you to the Pep-Terranova fight at the Garden."

Having never been to Madison Square Garden, the idea of attending a fight there, with Roth, widened my eyes. And there was no way to stay cool about it as I reached out and pumped his hand vigorously. "It's a deal."

"Good. Now we've got something to work for."

Right then I considered admitting the whole ball of wax to him, figuring if I couldn't trust the lieutenant, who could I trust? But that wasn't the point. I was too worried what a confession might do to Miss Porter. So I remained quiet and said goodbye.

Fortunately, Roth dropped me off a block away from the store. If my father had seen me leave the car, there would have been trouble for certain. Although my mother was confident I was safe with the detective, both my folks were still in the dark about my real involvement with the case. And I knew that if my father found out that I was moonlighting as a detective, there was no doubt he'd have me spending several months in solitary, or at least until my bar mitzvah.

16

Roth and I had reached an agreement which allowed me the weekends off. So when Saturday finally rolled around, I had some time to do a little investigating on the sly.

Gathering the necessary gear for my mission, I toyed with the idea of taking along my Jack Armstrong Decoder. Already packed was my Frank Buck Explorer's Sun Watch with the built-in compass, plus my Jack Armstrong Pedometer and Whistling Ring—all essentials. The decoder did seem a bit frivolous, but at the last moment I grabbed it, just in case.

I made my way by bicycle towards Heinz's gray shingled house on Cooke Street. Passing Keller Plastic and Smith's Pond, I spotted a couple of kids without skates playing makeshift hockey with branches and a small rock for a puck. My father's warning about "thin ice" and the accompanying stories of kids falling through and drowning, were obviously a classic example of parental exaggeration. I'd never actually heard about anyone falling through, and those guys sure looked safe enough out there. It always seemed to me like all the kids south of the tracks were never harassed or nagged by parents. They went mostly undisciplined and untended, giving them free reign on adventure. My adventure, on the other hand, was usually stolen. Still, I took what I could get.

Buddy and I had passed Heinz's house a hundred times on our bikes, occasionally tossing around the idea of messing his place up with eggs or paint, but we never found the nerve. If we had known then how fearsome Big Lew truly was, we'd never have even considered it.

According to my mother—and she was very dependable about town trivia—Heinz acquired his house and a couple of others in the neighborhood from some old con who'd been sent up years earlier for embezzling. With Wentworth's help, Heinz helped reduce the crook's sentence and was able to pick up the properties for next to nothing. As far as anyone knew, Big Lew rented them out—with Keller's cooperation—to factory workers who moved in from out of town, then probably split the money with the mayor.

Hardly anyone was around the area as I made my way up Cooke Street. Nevertheless, I got off my bike and started pushing, hoping to keep a low profile. Approaching Heinz's place, I was surprised to spot that mysterious Olds coupe parked in the dirt driveway. Usually Big Lew had the patrol car parked there, but I assumed that had already been impounded. From behind a truck parked curbside, I studied the coupe, which was dark green and slightly battered. My guess was 1940, not that I was an expert. The Connecticut license plate was RK-4381. I made a mental note.

As I was about to ride off, the side door to the house swung open and Avery Wentworth strolled out, then climbed into the Olds on the passenger side.

A moment later, another man, looking vaguely familiar, came out of the house. He was tall, and wore a brown crumpled suit. His gray stetson was pulled down low and his trousers were a little short. Getting behind the wheel of the coupe, he started it up after a couple of tries, then jerked out of the driveway and headed off down the street, nearly sideswiping an oncoming truck.

Then, the door of the house opened again. This time it was Heinz's oddball mother. I'd seen her around town before. She certainly wasn't the sweet old lady who baked pies for her kid on Sundays. In fact, I can still remember the first time I saw her, she had wandered into our store to shop. She poked around for twenty minutes muttering in some strange language before leaving in a huff and calling the place a "pigsty."

When she crossed the street, I decided to tail her. It crossed my mind that maybe she was mixed up in her son's dirty work, if not the ring leader. She was wearing a perfect disguise: black coat, a peculiar hat with a veil, and laced matronly shoes. She even carried her own shopping net. This, I reasoned, was to make a pickup of top secret information somewhere in town. Dogging her on my bike, I stayed about fifty feet behind. I'd already determined she must be packing a piece. Just in case, I had my Whistling Ring clutched in my fist ready to blow.

Suddenly, Mrs. Heinz slipped into Wheeler's Market. It was smaller than Silver's General and specialized in meats and produce. My parents didn't look upon Wheeler as a competitor. They were fond of the old-timer and always offered him a soda whenever he dropped in at Silver's. So when I asked what Mrs. Heinz purchased, Wheeler happily confided that she'd bought six sausages, apples and Maxwell House Coffee—all the while complaining about the prices.

I caught up and followed her back to the house, then waited awhile. Anxious to make my report, I finally raced home and excitedly called Roth. Luckily, his wife caught him just as he was leaving.

"Good work," Roth said. "I don't know about the grocery list, but the license plate is valuable info, partner."

After I hung up, a grin as big as the quarter moon lit up my face. I'd done my first real leg-work and made my first official contribution to the case. Roth had said he'd "run a make" on the Olds' license. I loved that phrase. It sounded like the stuff I'd heard on "Mr. District Attorney." The best part, though, was being called "partner."

❧

By mid-afternoon, Buddy and I were determined to get some football going at the ballfield. Unfortunately, we couldn't dig up enough kids for a game. Alan Birdwell wanted to play, but when he learned that it might be tackle, he backed off. And it was a good thing. Birdwell got on my nerves enough during school. Given the chance to grind him into the dirt, I would have happily done so, which surely would've meant a nasty call from Mrs. Birdwell to my parents.

With football out, I asked Buddy if he had any cigarettes so the day wouldn't be a total loss. Scrounging in his pockets, he came up with one pathetic-looking butt that he offered to share. At least we were spending time together.

We lit up and camped out on the picnic table—the same one on which Bondi and Miss Porter had writhed and moaned. That day seemed years away, like a vague dream. But the thing I vividly remembered, still remember even, was the way Bondi's hand slid up that soft thigh en route to those black panties.

"Mary Beth's some beauty," I said, faking a long drag. Concerned with keeping in shape for sports, I never inhaled.

"Mary Beth? Cut the crap," Buddy smirked. "You don't call her that."

"Just when we're alone," I teased, "after school." Although I hadn't actually worked up the courage to call her Mary Beth, I was hoping Buddy would buy that story all the same. "She calls me Zack," I said. "And I call her Mary Beth." I tried to sound cool. "She says I've got talent."

"I'll bet she says that to Big Lew, too."

"Screw you!"

Buddy flicked his cigarette down and stomped it out. "What are you giving her for Christmas, Romeo, a self-portrait?"

I was tempted to belt him—but thinking about it, that didn't seem like such a bad idea.

17

Every Saturday night I took a long, hot bath. School days were always too hectic to squeeze in an hour of solid washing "behind the ears and between the toes," as my mother insisted. Saturday then, was appropriately called "Scrub Night" at the Silvers.

While soaking in the tub, I considered taking in a movie with Buddy. "State Fair" was playing at the Bartlett and he had been frothing to see Jeanne Craine "up real close." Buddy was of the opinion that she looked "sorta like Melissa," but I told him I'd already seen enough of her at school and would rather stay home and catch "Your Hit Parade."

The radio was set out in the hallway with the volume turned way up; my mother never allowed me to take the table model into the bathroom, afraid I'd fry myself by dropping it in the tub. So I usually resorted to keeping the door ajar and killing the lights.

Relaxing in the dark, I pictured Miss Porter as Doris Day singing "The More I See You," currently *Number Two*. The warm water felt soothing and I imagined Miss Porter warbling the hit especially for me, her greatest fan and would-be lover. Soon, I was mouthing the lyrics with Doris and swaying in the suds. By the time the song ended, my heart was pounding. I reached over, dripping soapy water, and locked the door. But the ringing telephone interrupted my dreams.

"Zachary . . . call!" my mother yelled.

"Who is it?"

"It was Lieutenant Roth!"

"*Was?*"

She'd already hung up. "I don't think your father would appreciate your getting calls from the lieutenant."

I didn't appreciate it either, at least not in the middle of a torrid fantasy.

"Why's the light off in there?"

I could see her shadow checking the crack under the door.

"Zachary, are you and Buddy in trouble again?"

I let the water drain from the tub and quickly dried myself. Slipping into my robe, I switched on the light and opened the door.

"Why do you always think I'm in trouble?" I said, heading for my bedroom with my mother right on my heels.

Planting herself at my doorway she took a deep breath and folded her arms. "Exactly what is going on, Zachary?"

"Exactly nothing."

"You've been acting very peculiar lately, spending odd hours out all the time." She paused, but only for a moment. "And Buddy must call here three times a day trying to catch up with you."

"I'm busy," I said, sitting at my desk and cracking open my math book.

"I'm your mother, Zachary, and I happen to know when something is wrong with my baby."

I never really minded her lectures, but when she called me her "baby," it never failed to set me off.

"Look, Mom," I said. "I'm practically a teenager. And according to Jewish law, almost a man." She sighed as I continued. "I've already got a ton of things to do, what with regular school and six extra hours of Hebrew school a week. So if I say I'm busy, it's because I *am*. And I've told Buddy that a hundred times. I don't know why he calls so much."

"I understand all that," she said. "But it still doesn't explain your getting so involved with this detective business."

"It's just because I'm familiar with what's going on around town, I've been helping the lieutenant out a little. Telling him what I know about certain people and stuff."

After my spiel, she appeared to relax, even smile. And eying my math book, she said, "Well, I'm glad to see you getting a good start on your schoolwork for Monday." Then she left.

I was forever amazed that my mother never hounded Lenny like she did me. God knows, there was plenty for her to worry about, what with Lenny's totally aimless lifestyle; he'd roll in just before dinner on weekends without any explanation, eat, then disappear without a word. My father dubbed him the "Saturday Evening Ghost."

"Saturday's a big night," Lenny had confided to me. "A couple of guys always come into the alley who like to gamble. I stay in the back, see, and knock down a few pins for them by kicking the reset-button. Then afterwards, the guys meet me outside and cut me in on their take." And to think my mother used to say Lenny was "such a nice boy."

Since Lenny started working at the bowling alley, I

more or less had free rein of the airwaves on weekends. Except when it came to the Heatter newscasts
which my father insisted on hearing—or the melo-
dramas my mother liked crying over. After "Your Hit
Parade" came "Truth or Consequences," a perennial
favorite of mine. Then after "Truth . . . ," I could
look forward to "The F.B.I. in Peace and War," naturally hoping to pick up some pointers on
investigating.

When the radio shows ended I went into my bedroom. Closing the door quietly, I shuffled through
the bottom drawer of my desk for my Jack Armstrong
paraphernalia, taking careful inventory on the gadgets tucked into the secret pockets I'd cut in my
jacket lining. Like Jack always said, "There's nothing
more important than being prepared." But nothing
could have prepared me for the next couple of days.

18

Almost everybody in Oakville dressed up on Sundays. That was "Church and Chow Day" according to Buddy, the day most people ate out. Families either had breakfast at May's Diner, lunch at Quinlan's, or dinner and drinks at Gino's Bar and Grill. Some families with money, like the Kellers, often enjoyed a meal at each place, maybe switching the order every week for variety.

Being a Jewish boy in a town of gentiles, I never had quite the same social opportunities as the other kids. Only on Yom Kippur and a couple of other High Holy Days did our family dress up and trek into Waterbury for services at the Temple Beth Zion, and we rarely ate at any of the restaurants. I never understood why, but the Silvers didn't socialize as a family at local functions; my father said there just wasn't any time. And both my parents were somewhat against Lenny's or my getting involved with non-Jewish kids, especially girls. But seeing as kids have to have friends and the Keller children weren't my idea of a good time, my parents accepted Buddy and Melissa the best they could. Still, I wonder why, as an "oppressed minority," our family never made any effort to integrate.

There was one time I even asked my father if being Jewish meant "being superior."

"You're a smart kid, Zack," he said. "It's not that we think we're better than others. But the Talmud does say that Jews are the chosen people." And I could tell my father wanted to keep it that way.

The older I got, the more I began to realize that my restricted religious upbringing only made me more attracted to the likes of Miss Porter, Melissa Edwards and Ingrid Bergman—the ultimate WASPS. These were, of course, women my parents would have preferred I didn't mix with; obviously they had nothing to worry about with Ingrid. But being something of a rebel, I found waspish women all the more interesting for just that reason. My mother's unending enthusiasm for Cindy Keller was one of the chief reasons Cindy didn't interest me, despite her bobbed nose and blonde-streaked hair. It was more fun to like what you aren't supposed to like and generally contradict your parents' wishes—at least that's what Lenny always taught me.

Buddy had gone to a late Mass that Sunday morning, so by the time we met at Smith's Pond, it was mid-afternoon. The day was brisk and gray, and we wanted to test the ice along with the other kids. It seemed solid enough, but I didn't have the nerve to venture more than a few feet beyond the shore.

"Next week I'm going to ask my folks if I can skate."

"My old man doesn't give a damn if I skate out here in July."

I couldn't tell if Buddy was bragging about his independence or complaining about his father's indifference.

Heading back to Buddy's house on our bikes, I spotted the mysterious Olds coupe parked in the shadows on the auxiliary road under the trestle. I held my hand out and put my finger to my lips, not unlike John Wayne spearheading the ambush in "Back to Bataan." We camouflaged our bikes behind some brush and advanced quietly and slowly, taking cover behind a nearby boulder.

"What's up?" Buddy asked.

"Shhhh!"

Hunkering in the scrub, we were close enough to see Big Lew at the Olds' wheel with Miss Porter alongside him on the passenger side. They were arguing about something. But as the car windows were closed, their battle wasn't audible. Miss Porter, face flushed and tearful, was flailing her arms and shouting. Heinz was less animated, tight-lipped and tense. I didn't want to watch, but I couldn't turn away either.

"He's really got a way with women," Buddy whispered sarcastically.

I could only shake my head.

Suddenly, Miss Porter burst from the car in tears. Big Lew sprang out after her. She began to run through the knee-high shrubbery, but Heinz caught her from behind, spun her around and clamped onto her shoulders. She struggled, kicking and writhing, then spit in his face. "Let go! I hate you!" she screamed.

But he wouldn't release her. He just wiped the spit from his cheek onto his shirt and grinned menacingly. "Shut up, bitch!"

"You bastard," she said. *"I hate you!"*

Heinz muffled her mouth with one of his enormous paws. "As long as you keep your trap shut," he said, "I don't care what you think."

Her eyes narrowed and she hissed, "I should have

just let you arrest me. Prison would've been better than this!''

"You wouldn't have lasted one day in the pen," Heinz said, chuckling. "They would've eaten you alive."

I didn't know what they were talking about, and turned to Buddy confused. He shrugged his shoulders slowly in mesmerized fascination.

Then, Miss Porter wrenched an arm free and slapped Heinz's smiling mug. It was a hard, angry whack that echoed in the gully.

Heinz went purple with rage. You could see his neck swell up and he started snorting like a bull. "You little slut!"

"Fuck off!" Then she kicked him hard in the shins.

Grasping her wrists with one strong fist, Big Lew hauled off and whacked her with the back of his right hand, sending her tumbling into the weeds.

I started to lunge forward, but someone, a lot stronger than Buddy, grabbed me from behind. I whirled around. It was Roth, whose look instantly told me to shut up and stay cool. I did, and when I looked back, Miss Porter had gotten up and was running off hysterically. Heinz stormed into the coupe muttering curses, slammed the door and roared off in a spray of dust.

"We couldn't have done anything," Roth said. "This isn't our business."

"When did you get here?"

"Just a minute ago," he said. "I saw your bikes in the bushes. Didn't hide them very well . . ." He glanced at Buddy, no doubt wondering just how much I'd already told him.

"How did you know they were *our* bikes?" Buddy asked.

"I recognized Zack's from the other day."

"Did you see Big Lew's car?" I asked. "That's the one I was talking about."

"I know," Roth said. "I checked the DMV and the Olds is registered to Lewis G. Heinz."

Since I'd never seen Heinz in the car, besides that day at the hospital when someone picked him up, I was perplexed. But I kept it to myself. "I'd better see if Miss Porter's all right," I suggested.

"I'll do that," Roth said. "I'd rather you see if the Olds turns up back at Heinz's house."

I wasn't thrilled with that assignment.

"Go on. You can do it on the way home," Roth said.

Buddy nudged me. "Let's go, Zack."

Roth, already on his way to find Miss Porter, shouted back, "I'll call you later, kid!"

As we retrieved our bikes from the scrub, Buddy shook his head. "I don't like that guy, Zack."

"Jealous again?"

Buddy smirked. "Yeah sure, I'd love it. Roth always hanging on my neck."

"He's just keeping an eye on me 'cause he thinks I know something."

"Looks like he's keeping his other eye on Miss Porter."

I mounted my bike and started pedalling fast, making it tough for Buddy and his bent rim to catch up. He called for me to wait up, but I didn't. I just pedalled faster and faster—almost wishing I could ride right out of town.

19

During art class the following day, I couldn't help but notice the bruise on Miss Porter's cheek, which she had tried unsuccessfully to cover with makeup. I attempted to catch her gaze, let her know I understood, but our eyes didn't meet once during the entire period. Knowing who had damaged that gorgeous face got me so upset I couldn't draw without chipping off huge pieces of my charcoal.

We were supposed to be sketching Evette LaBeck, who was posing in some skimpy peasant costume. I would have preferred drawing Miss Porter or Melissa. Evette, looking awkward and embarrassed, no doubt would have preferred the same. She kept trying to stick out her chest and suck in her belly, making it tough for me to sketch her and almost impossible not to snicker.

Miss Porter had given us all large sheets of paper and what seemed like lumps of soft coal. It was a mess. I purposely drew my sketch out of proportion, hoping she would lean over to help me. I was craving a noseful of her lilac scent. But when she finally came to my drawing, she merely glanced at it, nodded approval and moved on to Buddy's stick figure rendering, where extra assistance was required.

As the day plodded on, I suffered through Latin, history and the other boring subjects which were supposed to be shaping my mind. Instead, my imagination took over and I found myself unconsciously doodling in my notebook, drawing countless variations of blood-stained daggers. Nothing seemed to matter anymore. Nothing except solving the case.

Staring out the window during English class, I noticed Miss Porter race off to teach music at the high school. She peeled her Ford out of the parking lot faster than usual. How I wished I was in the front seat with her. I wouldn't have cared where we went, just as long as there were only the two of us and no Heinz. If she bothered to ask me, though, I probably would've suggested Brooklyn so we could enjoy Ebbets Field together.

Before I realized it, the school bell had sounded and all the kids were barreling out into the fresh cool air. Unfortunately, I had Hebrew school to contend with. As expected, Roth was waiting for me in the Packard. I told him I'd try to get back to Oakville in time to do a little gumshoeing before dinner, but he was quick to remind me that it was getting dark earlier now. I offered to skip Hebrew School just this once, but he cut me off before I could even finish my sentence.

"Don't worry, it's more important that you go." I was secretly hoping Roth would accept my offer. "Temple Beth Zion is a fine synagogue," he said. "My family are members of the congregation."

Actually, I didn't care if slugger Hank Greenberg was a member; I just didn't like having to spend two or three hours there learning stuff I didn't understand. I could think of a hundred things I'd rather be doing. Worst of all, my arms were getting soft from all the recent inactivity and I knew it would take at least a month of solid playing just to get my shooting eye back. But then I thought about it, and realized that with Coach Ryan in the clink—what was the point?

Corky Pope, who took over for Coach Ryan, was not motivating. Gangly and loud, Pope was unable to inspire us to move during practice without yelling. And when he wasn't hollering, he was telling everyone how great he was at their age.

Corky's sole claim to athletic fame was that he'd won a basketball scholarship to the University of Connecticut after an "outstanding year," as he put it, playing center for Warren Harding High in Bridgeport. But rumor had it that when Corky tried to compete in college, the big fellas from the industrial towns effortlessly manhandled him. Whether it was true or not, none of the kids ever took Pope seriously. It wasn't that Coach Ryan had such a great player-record himself, but at least he barked with authority and got results. And he had a sense of humor, something Pope sorely lacked. The more I thought about Coach Ryan, the more I missed him. Not just for basketball, but I enjoyed seeing him strolling the halls at lunch, trading insults with the school jocks. Ryan always had a comeback, and I liked that. If only everything hadn't come down to a choice between Coach Ryan or Miss Porter, maybe that twelfth year of my life wouldn't have been so traumatic.

According to Mr. Goodson, Ryan had hired some hotshot lawyer from New Haven. The murder trial was set for early January right after the holidays and just before my bar mitzvah. Everyone knew that

Heinz was plenty nervous, although he never showed it, what with that damned smug expression of his.

"I wish I could just turn the calendar ahead a couple of months and have Big Lew behind bars," I said.

Roth saw it differently. "No, we need time for things to unfold naturally," he said. "And I don't want to scare Heinz into doing anything rash. That could be very dangerous."

That got me thinking. And I recalled the time Buddy squealed under pressure from the school principal, admitting that *we* were the ones who tossed the stink bombs in Assembly. I remembered how surprised I was that he confessed so easily and suddenly worried that if Buddy was pressured, he'd blab everything. I could just imagine Buddy's words spilling out all at once, like he was puking. But I also knew that he was my best friend, and if he had already been milked for the information, he'd have surely confessed to me right away so we could both catch the next train to Alaska. Or so I prayed.

❧

I returned from Waterbury and Hebrew school too late to meet Roth; another day ruined by my heritage, was all I could think. Also, Lenny had arrived ten minutes earlier and already controlled the newspaper and bathroom.

Lenny informed me that the movie at the Bartlett

had changed and tonight would be the start of a picture that was "strictly adult." I didn't know quite what that meant, but it sounded interesting enough. Gathering my courage, I told my mother that I'd finished all my homework and asked if I could go— even though it was a school night.

"I don't know, Zack. You look like you could use some sleep."

Taking a different approach, I decided not to argue. And in the end, she said, "Okay, as long as you come right home when the movie's over."

While Brylcreeming my hair, I studied myself in the bathroom mirror. I did look tired and rundown. After all, I hadn't been in the sun much and had been exposed to an adult dose of pressure. Running my fingers over my face, I hunted for a trace of stubble. I'd have done anything for that he-man Gable look. Actually, I was already making plans for a moustache—Lenny claimed they made noses look smaller—and had picked out several styles from magazine ads that I admired. I actually considered questioning Rabbi Glick as to why the Jews were the people "chosen" to have big noses.

Eventually, I called Buddy and said I'd meet him in front of the theatre at seven o'clock. I'd conned both my mother and him into thinking that the movie was "National Velvet." Only I knew the picture was "The Lost Weekend," supposedly that "adult" drama Lenny had recommended.

Heading towards the Bartlett, I realized that all those stories about having your childhood come and go at the speed of lightning were actually happening to me—and I didn't like it.

I plunked down sixty-five cents at the box office window and was annoyed to see that "The Lost Weekend" was starting *tomorrow*. By now, Buddy had bought his sweets and was waiting inside. Never believe Lenny, I thought.

I told Buddy that I wasn't interested in seeing "National Velvet," but that I just had to get out of the house for some fun. He seconded my reasoning. So we bought some candy and settled into our usual seats near the side exit. The year before, we'd carved our initials in the armrests.

After a Pathe newsreel which showed the happy return of soldiers from war, a Popeye cartoon and Coming Attractions, the feature started. By then, I'd polished off all my goodies and was feeling sick to my stomach.

Needless to say, "National Velvet" was a lemon. It was a soapy story about some butcher's daughter and a bum kid who train a horse to win the Grand National over in England. But I will admit that I was struck by Elizabeth Taylor's pretty face and eyes, which vaguely resembled Melissa's. I even closed my eyes for a few moments imagining Melissa next to me in the dark, snuggled up on my shoulder. But when I glanced over, there was Buddy, jawing on his third candy bar.

After the show we set off in separate directions. It was cold and windy outside as I made my way towards the apartment. As I turned the corner down Maple Street, a strong wind knocked over a garbage can in my path. Shivering and afraid, I longed for the safety of my bed as the trees, swaying back and forth in the wind, cast ominous shadows. Dark objects appeared to be darting in and out of alleys and behind cars. Finally, I started counting aloud to keep from panicking. Then I lost track at number fifteen or sixteen and my heart began pounding. Another pail crashed down behind me and I sprinted the rest of the way home. I probably looked like a jerk—but every shadow looked like Big Lew.

20

Our Frigidaire contained one uncooked chicken, an old piece of cheese, half an apple and a third of a bottle of milk minus the cream. "The Baum" had struck again, and my stomach ached for something to soothe my insides. Of course, there was always Dole's. But I settled for some watery milk and a stale slice of Wonder Bread with raspberry jam, which made me feel even worse.

I tossed and turned in bed for what seemed like hours trying to fall asleep. Then, just as I was dozing off, the phone rang. I sprang out to the hallway to grab it before everyone woke up. "Hello?" I whispered.

"It's me." The caller was Roth.

My mother instantly shouted from my parents' bedroom. "Who is it, Zachary?"

I called back in a half-whisper. "It's Buddy. He . . . uh, lost his wallet."

She seemed to buy it because the shouting stopped.

"It's midnight for cryin' out loud. What's going on?"

"I'm worried," Roth said. "Miss Porter just told me that Heinz knows Buddy was around school the afternoon of the murder."

All of a sudden the surrounding walls and bolted door didn't seem strong enough to restrain Big Lew. I gulped and wondered if he was also aware that *I* was with Buddy. Because if he did, I knew I had a train to catch. "W-What do you think we should do?"

"Just keep an eye on Buddy. That's all we can do for now. I'll talk to Miss Porter again tomorrow and find out more. Sorry I had to call so late. Go back to bed."

After he hung up, I had a vision of Roth telling her that the only reason he was associating with me was because he suspected I was withholding vital information. Then I heard footsteps. Roth's news was something I didn't need to hear before trying to get in a solid night's sleep. I realized I couldn't call Buddy—Mr. Goodson would have a cow. On the other hand, I couldn't go to bed knowing that my best friend was probably next on Big Lew's hit list. What's more, I didn't understand what Roth was doing at Miss Porter's place after midnight.

Crawling back into bed, I felt sick and shaky and lay there with my eyes open, heart thumping. I snapped the radio on, and extending the cord into bed, pulled the covers up and over me and the radio, then turned the volume down low. It wasn't uncommon after troublesome nights for my father to discover me the following morning snuggled in bed with the radio still playing. Luckily, he was understanding about this and never mentioned it to my mother, who surely would have lectured me about conserving energy.

The radio news was still on, and according to the announcer, the U.S. was decreasing its military strength and would soon be cutting its armed forces at the rate of a million men a month. By March, the newscaster said, the world's greatest air force would be down to 150,000 men.

I was finally beginning to drift off to sleep when the news ended and gave way to music. After Harry James' rendition of "It's Been a Long, Long Time," they played "Till The End Of Time," sung by Perry Como. It was slow and schmaltzy, and sent me floating off on yet another dream date with Miss Porter and her silky black panties.

⌒✶

Next day before classes, Buddy and I saw Popovich limping down the hallway—his left arm in a sling, his head bandaged. Poor guy looked like he'd been hit by a blitzkrieg. No one dared ask Popovich what had happened. The teachers all gave him some light homework assignments and he was excused for the day. Seeing Popovich so bashed up really got to me. And there was no doubt in my mind that Big Lew thought Popovich knew more than he first admitted and decided to work him over for a second helping of info.

It seemed like two whole days passed until recess came. Once we were outside, I told Buddy what Roth had reported. Buddy's face went sheet white. So I quickly changed the subject and started talking about the NHL standings. But he wasn't interested.

"How can I think about hockey at a time like this?"

I felt awful about it. But I couldn't help noticing

how this crisis was bringing us together again. I vowed to stick with Buddy through "thick or thin," though I wasn't exactly sure what the phrase meant. Finally, we made a pact that neither would go anywhere without the other. It was just like old times.

Later at glee club rehearsal, Miss Porter continued to avoid my eyes and I was beginning to get the feeling she was betraying me. I didn't mind the thought of her and Heinz, because after the Olds incident, I was convinced she hated him. But I wondered what she really thought of Roth and why she opened up to him so easily. And so late at night.

After school I asked Buddy to wait for me outside. "I've gotta talk to Miss Porter about something."

He looked at me suspiciously. "What about our pact?"

"Just wait, dammit!"

It was the second time that day I'd bit someone's head off; the morning had begun in similar fashion. At breakfast my mother blamed me for wasting electricity with my all-night radio. Then Maibaum jumped in with details about how the planet would be doomed without energy by the year 1980 if people like me "wasted just two megawatts of energy each day." That was all it took for me to tear into Maibaum about him skimming the cream off the top of the milk when he didn't even buy it. After that, the table was silent, and I got some strange stares from Lenny and my mother.

Miss Porter wasn't in the Art Room, so I checked outside in the picnic area. Finally, I found her under the oak tree having a smoke. As I approached, she took a deep drag on her Chesterfield and exhaled slowly. This was the designated smoking area for teachers. It had also been the scene of the crime.

"I have to ask you something," I said, trying to sound like an investigator.

"Go ahead, shoot." She still hadn't looked into my eyes.

"Did Heinz beat up Popovich yesterday?"

She snuffed the cigarette in the dirt and started back inside. I tagged alongside. I could tell her manner with me was different, sort of distracted and distant.

"There's no other way Big Lew could have found out Buddy was around school that afternoon," I said, "unless he beat it out of Popovich."

She paused, turned, and finally met my eyes. "I know how close you are to Buddy, Zack, and I'm really sorry he's being pulled into this. But I don't understand why you're getting mixed up with Lieutenant Roth in this investigation."

"Maybe he needs me."

She looked at me curiously. But I could tell she was really concerned. "The important thing is that neither of you get hurt," she said.

There she goes again, I thought, worrying about Roth. "I'm not some stupid kid, you know. I can take care of myself."

"Of course you can," she said, with a slight smile. "But then again, so can Officer Heinz."

"I'm not scared of that big goon."

She spoke softly. "Well, I am, Zack."

I followed her back to school, neither one of us talking. When I got to the front steps we said goodbye and that was that. Buddy had already left. I figured he'd gotten bored and headed home for a snack. I was hustling to catch up with him when Roth's car cut me off. I didn't hesitate climbing inside. He was exactly the person I wanted to talk to. The snack could wait.

"Can we take a ride over to Black Rock?" I said.

Roth just glanced at me, then shifted into first gear and pulled out of the parking lot. On the drive out of town towards the lake, neither of us said a word. Roth's eyes checked the rearview mirror. I sat rigidly, looking forward. "Take a right over here," I said.

Slowing, he turned onto a dirt roadway edging the pond. Black Rock, usually occupied by happy swimmers and picnickers in warm weather, was now deserted. "You can park there, under those pines," I said, indicating a shadowy area at the side of the road. Roth pulled to a stop and turned off the ignition. We sat silently, but it was as though he knew exactly what was coming. I had my gaze fixed on the little star of David as I began. I didn't want Miss Porter getting hurt anymore. And I wanted Big Lew behind bars, even if that meant testifying.

"Heinz did it," I blurted. "I saw the whole thing." My voice wavered. "He shoved a knife into Bondi's belly and . . . and twisted it around and around." The words came with surprising ease, racing up from my gut. The truth was out and I felt like a new person.

My eyes suddenly filled with tears and my body started shaking with sobs. A tremendous sense of relief rushed through my body in a wave. I was breathing in air as though I'd just come up from the bottom of the lake. The image of Big Lew and the knife being turned in living flesh was still strong in my mind.

Roth remained still, but his eyes widened and he exhaled slowly. "Good guy," he said calmly, placing a hand on my shoulder. "Did you see what Heinz did with the knife?"

I thought back. "Yeah, he tossed it into the bushes next to that big oak."

"Good," Roth said. "I already got it to the lab boys."

Obviously, he was checking out my story. Getting the secret out of my system was a relief, but it was only temporary. Realizing I was the sole witness and that I'd told everything sank in all too fast. And I could picture Big Lew's twitching jowls and enraged glare.

We sat quietly a long time, Roth's hand gently patting my shoulder until my sobbing stopped. Taking my chin firmly, he looked me square in the eyes and said, "Don't tell anyone else about this, okay?"

I swallowed and held my breath, wondering if that meant Buddy, too. Then my eyes shifted to the sound of an approaching vehicle. It was the town police car with the big number "17" plastered on its side. I quickly scooted down out of sight. Roth sat calmly as the patrol car passed.

"I think it was just a deputy," Roth said. Then he faced me again. "You can be of tremendous help to me, Zachary. This is a very important case."

"You aren't gonna tell about what I saw are you?" I asked, sitting up.

"Neither of us is going to say a word," he said. "I have a plan. But it requires absolute confidence on both our parts. You've got to trust me as much as I trust you, Zachary. And if you want to talk, you come talk to me.''

I felt a lot safer now with someone besides Buddy on my side. "Won't the knife prove Big Lew's guilt?"

"Unfortunately, there were no fingerprints," Roth said. "It's your testimony that'll prove Coach Ryan's innocence, Zachary. But I need to have another talk with Ryan so he understands the situation.''

Despite the gravity of the situation, I couldn't help feeling a little excited, like I was suddenly on "Gangbusters." "Call me Zack if you want," I said, managing a grin.

"Zack it is," Roth agreed.

21

Life Magazine was another treat Lenny monopolized —only giving the old one up when the latest one arrived. The November 12, '45 issue featured a gorgeous cover photo of Ingrid Bergman. She had been named Star Of The Year, having filmed "Saratoga Trunk," "Spellbound," and "The Bells of St. Mary's." I was amazed by her striking resemblance to Miss Porter.

Home sick that day with a sore throat, I bested Lenny by grabbing the magazine first. I loved *Life*, and particularly enjoyed the Letters to Editors section, which I always scanned to see if any celebrities had written in. So I was delighted to find a note from a lady about a previous cover story on her famous son.

> The *Life* picture story of my boy,
> Jimmy, was superb. I'll cherish it always.
> Bessie Stewart

I had secretly hoped that one day I could've given my mother occasion to write in about *her* son.

> *Life's* story of my son, Zachary, was wonderful. Even when he was a boy, I knew Zack was special. I'm glad he's been able to share his artistic talent with the rest of the world.
> Reva Silver

Being ill had other rewards as well. It provided me with the opportunity to be alone with my father, who enjoyed showering me with all sorts of surprises from the store—sweets, toys and comic books.

Compared with my father, my mother and I spent little time together—except for those rides back from Waterbury where most of her energy was exhausted maneuvering the "Silvermobile." We did, however, go together to see "Oklahoma" on Broadway once. It was a matinee, and by the time we had returned by train to Waterbury, it was almost midnight. She loved the choreography and couldn't stop talking about the show for weeks. Naturally, I was more impressed with the souvenirs sold during intermission, not to mention the stunning chorus girls.

With me laid up, my mother relieved my father in the store before leaving for yet another meeting with our lawyer in Waterbury. So my father came upstairs and we had cups of tea with honey. Sitting on the edge of my bed and sipping quietly, my father's expression soon tightened. Then, he started in: "Your mother and I are very concerned, Zack."

"About what?" I said, feigning innocence.

"I know all about his background, but this business with you and Lieutenant Roth and the investigation has me terribly worried. I'm afraid your mother and I don't see eye to eye on this."

Usually my father and mother agreed on how to deal with me, but this went down in Silver family history as "The Great Rift."

"Don't worry, Dad. I'm not in any danger." His look remained determinedly disapproving.

"You're getting involved with a *murder investigation*, Zachary."

Whenever my full name was attached to the end of a sentence, it was a bad sign. "Just what is this Lieutenant Roth *after*?" he asked, gazing at me unblinking.

"He's just taken over the case from Big Lew," I said. "And he's asking the kids from school a few questions. He's Jewish." I thought that last bit of info would appeal to my father. But he kept peering at me skeptically. "And he's got this really nice wife and twin daughters."

My father sipped his tea while I scrounged up one more tidbit: "And they belong to Temple Beth Zion. Isn't that great?"

But I was striking out.

He stopped drinking his tea. "I'll be honest with you, Zachary." Another bad sign. "I *don't want you involved in this thing*. It's simply too dangerous for someone your age."

For perhaps the first time, I realized that my father wasn't so unaware after all, and that he and my mother communicated a great deal more than I figured. I almost told my father that this was a helluva way to treat a sick person—but the conversation was undeniably over. He patted me on the knee, rose, and disappeared into the hallway without another word. Even my mother couldn't reason with him when he sank into his silent mode.

I lay in bed raging to myself that I was a young *man*, and that I could make my own decisions. Not that I wanted to be a man just yet, but if I was going to have the responsibilities of manhood, I wanted to enjoy the benefits. I now realize, though, that my father's concern was not only for my well-being, but also for his son's affection. No parent enjoys having their child spend more time with a stranger than with themselves.

After five minutes of muted fury, I rolled over onto my stomach and fell into one of those deep afternoon sleeps.

I was hurtling through some dark tunnel stark naked. And as I soared into a vast open space, the air became warm and balmy. Up ahead, there was a dim glow. Then, I landed in a soft field of moss and began walking towards the lush forest in the distance. But my journey was very difficult because deep chasms and crevices abruptly opened in my path, forcing me to leap over them one at a time. Each hurdle took all my strength and every time I felt I couldn't go on, another gap would crack open, longer and deeper than the last.

Suddenly a huge man, wearing a black football uniform with a big number 17 plastered on his jersey, appeared from out of nowhere and clipped me from the side. Toppling into the darkness of a massive crevice, I dropped straight to the bottom. I struggled to climb out. My lungs pinched tightly and my breath grew short. And although there was no water, it felt as though I was drowning.

Fortunately, a tall, bearded man in a flowing robe arrived and threw me a line so I could pull myself up. Making my way to the top, I passed a cottony nest containing three pearl-white eggs. I was hypnotized, but as I reached out to take one, I was startled by a commotion overhead. The big goon in the football uniform and the bearded man were locked in mortal combat, going for each other's throats.

Finally, the bruiser lifted the bearded man over his head and hurled him into the breach. As he tumbled past me, I realized that the bearded man was me, only older—myself as an old man. Inexplicably, I dove into the gully too.

I was sailing through space again, gasping for air, until I was jolted awake by the sound of a radio announcer:

"AND NOW . . . DICK TRACY!" Strange radio code signals swelled up full then slipped under the theme music. "Yes, folks, it's Dick Tracy. Protector of Law and Order . . ."

I opened my eyes and discovered that the announcer's voice was actually my brother's. It was 5:15 and Lenny had just arrived home.

"Get up you bum," he teased, yanking the pillow from under me.

"Leave me alone. I'm sick!"

"Yeah, sick in the head. Look at your pillow. You drooled all over it. You're worse than a dog."

My brother's cruelty never ceased to amaze me. The vivid and disturbing dream was still fresh in my mind and I felt miserable. I was hot and dizzy, so I asked Lenny to call Buddy and tell him I was too ill to go to our scout meeting that night. Lenny said he'd do it only if I'd give up all comic book rights and first choice of radio programs for two days.

I knew Lenny would make me pay for the measly favor one way or another, so I agreed and we shook on it. Nothing was binding with my brother unless there was a handshake involved. Lenny promptly announced that he wanted to hear "Mystery Theatre," knowing damn well I would have preferred "Inner Sanctum." But I'd already given up my vote.

Before dozing off again, I struggled to make sense of the peculiar dream. But there was no logic, no rhyme nor reason. Like the case itself, I had become a prisoner of fate, trapped in a web of confusion.

22

After sixteen hours of sleep I felt well enough to return to the relentless grind of school. Making my way towards Buddy's place in the morning I immediately noticed that the Goodson Studebaker was gone from the driveway and two unfamiliar sedans were parked out front.

Buddy's kid sister, Pam, eyes reddened from tears, was being escorted from the house by a tall man in a porkpie hat and topcoat. The man seemed particularly gentle and comforting as he ushered her into one of the parked sedans. I tried to catch Pam's attention as they drove away, waving both hands, but her eyes were downcast. I got the sudden feeling that something terrible had happened. Mr. Goodson must have suffered a heart attack, I concluded, and they've got him down at St. Luke's in Intensive Care. Obviously, Pam was being rushed to his side. The rest of the family had probably been there all night. All I could think was that Buddy should have called me.

As another man was about to get into the second car, I rushed over to ask what had happened. The man looked me over, then cleared his throat. "Buddy Goodson's in the hospital. He was found in some roadside bushes this morning. Looks like a hit and run."

My eyes dribbled out tears uncontrollably as a sense of dread overcame me. I had to see Buddy immediately. So I started racing towards St. Luke's.

131

The man tried to stop me, to call me back, but I wasn't listening. All I could hear was the screaming inside my head.

Though the road was familiar, I became totally disorientated. Instead of pausing to get my bearings, I kept running faster and faster. I couldn't get to the hospital quick enough. The physical activity relieved some of the pain, but it all seemed too crazy for logical thought. How could somebody run Buddy down and leave him on the roadside to die? I stopped to think it through, and I bit my finger to make sure it wasn't all another nightmare.

Then it hit me, hard, like I'd just been struck by a speeding car myself. The whole thing was my fault. If I hadn't gotten sick, Buddy and I would have gone to that scout meeting together. We probably would've gone for sodas afterwards and the few extra minutes might have prevented the disaster from ever happening. I remembered Roth telling me to keep an eye on Buddy. I remembered our pact never to go out alone at night. Suddenly, I found myself bawling in the middle of the road. I stood there, shoulders sagging, shaking my head thinking how much I loved Buddy Goodson.

After a few moments, I continued towards the hospital. But now I scurried, wiping the tears from my face as I ran. Certain images flashed in my mind: how Buddy and I had started kindergarten together as little kids; how competitive we were from the start; how we both had our eyes on Peg Murphy, a chubby little blonde who used to tie off her long braid with a pink ribbon, and how she dumped the pair of us in favor of Wentworth's great grandson.

Neither Buddy nor I ever mentioned it to anyone,

but that previous summer, when we were swimming at Black Rock alone, I was struck by a sharp cramp in the pit of my stomach and actually started to go under. I gulped in a lot of water and panicked. Within seconds I had blacked out and sunk slowly towards the bottom. Luckily, Buddy had grabbed me by the hair before it was too late. He'd hauled me to shore, and pressed my chest until I spat up and gasped back to life. From that point on, our bond became unbreakable and I knew that I owed Buddy everything. Although he knew how indebted I was, he never called me on it. He just seemed glad we were friends.

Shaken and bleary-eyed, it was hard for me to see more than a few yards ahead. But I trotted on, wishing the hospital would somehow meet me halfway. For a few hundred yards I even hoped that maybe *I'd* get hit by a truck or car, and that Buddy and I could be in adjoining hospital beds. My feelings ran the gamut, from hope and prayer that Buddy would be okay, to blind fury. But through it all I swore at the driver who struck him. I cursed everything and everyone that let this happen, primarily myself. My tears were no doubt mostly out of guilt.

When St. Luke's finally appeared in the distance, a sharp cramp seized my belly, wrenching more tears out. It was like I was drowning in my own misery. Stumbling the final hundred yards, I was overwhelmed by the smell of the hospital—that sickly, disinfectant odor. Entering the lobby, I spotted familiar faces and headed straight for Buddy's mother and Claire, who were huddled together in the waiting room.

Mrs. Goodson turned to me, her eyelids puffed

from crying. "Buddy's father is in there with Pam . . ." Then she broke down and embraced me, and we both wept openly. I tried to grab onto her for support, but she was shaking so badly I couldn't get a hold. A minute passed before she stopped sobbing and sputtered in my ear, "Buddy's in a c-coma." She paused, muffling another outburst. "They're not sure if he's going to make it."

I felt woozy and dug my fingers deep into her fleshy waist. My legs were wobbly and I had to take several deep breaths. Though I had already been told what had happened, I had to ask once again.

Mrs. Goodson tried to calm herself, swallowing a couple times. "Apparently, Buddy was walking home on Elmore after the scout meeting last night . . ." She was beginning to weep again, so Claire took over.

"Somebody hit him and just kept driving . . ."

I could picture Buddy lying there in pain all night, waiting for someone to find him. I kept thinking how much agony he must have suffered and wondered if I could ever take anything similar. I just wanted to tell Buddy what a terrific friend he was and that I'd never let him down again.

Mr. Goodson and Pam approached from the corridor. The sisters ran toward one another, embraced and shared another cry—as did Mr. and Mrs. Goodson, who held each other tightly. I needed someone to hold onto too. "Can I see him?"

Mr. Goodson, who gave me what seemed like an accusing look, nodded to the man in the suit down the corridor.

Composing myself, I approached the M.D. and asked if I could see Buddy.

"Okay, but you can only stay a few moments."

I couldn't believe I was asking some doctor I didn't know if I could visit my best friend in Intensive Care. With small, careful steps, I entered the room fearing even the slightest noise or bump might hurt my friend further. I forced a look. Buddy was a mass of bandages, splints and tubes. I fought tears and silently promised God that if my best friend pulled through and we were lucky enough to ever play together again, I'd let him beat me in one-on-one anytime he wanted. I also vowed that if he got better, I'd stop bitching about Hebrew school and be thankful every day of my life.

I realized I was making deals with someone I'd never wholly believed in before. But if Buddy survived, I knew there had to be someone up there who was taking care of things.

⚬❧

I got permission from my parents to skip Hebrew school that day, and after classes, I visited Buddy again. He was still unconscious—his face pale and sad, his body motionless. Buddy's folks and sisters had just left and I felt uneasy sitting alone in the darkened room listening to the blips of the heart monitor. What if something happens, if the monitor stops bleeping? What am I supposed to do? Without another thought, I rushed down the hallway and found the nearest nurse.

"What do I do if that machine turns off and I'm in there by myself?"

The nurse grabbed me by the shoulders. "It isn't going to stop. Okay?"

After several seconds, I nodded, embarrassed for having panicked. But the last thing I could've taken was seeing Buddy die right in front of me. There was just too much of myself wrapped up in my friend. I was convinced that his death would have killed a part of me as well.

Later, as I trudged from the hospital Roth pulled up in his Packard at the main entrance. He had obviously heard what had happened and knew exactly where to find me.

"Let's go for a ride," he said, placing a sympathetic hand on my shoulder.

I welcomed the idea of driving, hoping it might help me escape me from my troubles. We cruised around town for half an hour before either of us spoke.

"It's connected to the murder, you know," Roth said.

"I was just thinking that." I gazed out the window at the leafless trees. "Mrs. Goodson thinks it was some drunken driver."

Roth remained silent as we crossed the tracks and approached the factories. The day shift was letting out at Oakville Textile and we had to slow down for the workers. Everyone was rushing to their cars trying to get home and warm before dark.

We continued on, driving slowly and silently. Finally, we pulled to a stop across the street from Heinz's house. The driveway was empty. Roth killed the engine and we sat quietly watching through the trees. The kitchen light was on, and we could make out the silhouette of someone moving inside the house.

"You think Big Lew did it?" I asked.

"Or someone he hired."

It was all too confusing. I wanted facts, not speculation. I wanted justice. But the only thing I knew for certain was that Buddy was in the hospital and it seemed like the most unfair thing in the world.

23

Next day, Roth explained that we were going to stake out Heinz's place. "The key to this," he said, "is being patient. We wait for the right moment, then we pounce. It's cat and mouse from here on in."

"I say we just drop a bomb on his house."

Roth smirked, but he didn't realize how serious I was. My best friend had just been mowed down by the bastard that stabbed my history teacher, framed my coach and slapped around the great love of my life. How was I supposed to be patient?

"Maybe you'd better bring along a comic book," Roth suggested, "or something that'll keep you occupied for a couple of hours."

"I'm not taking my eyes off that house."

Because Heinz was familiar with the Packard, Roth obtained a Chevy loaner so we could watch the house from a parking spot down the street. Actually, Roth did the bulk of the watching, what with my busy schedule. But I made up for my end by bringing him a cheese sandwich, some apple pie and a thermos of milk from home.

"You're the best partner I've had," Roth said, wolfing down his snack.

"I figured you'd be hungry."

"You figured right."

I glanced over at Heinz's place. "Anything happen yet?"

Roth's mouth was full, so he could only shake his

head. But he managed to mumble, "Patience."

"Yeah yeah, I know."

Taking a final swig from the thermos, Roth informed me that he'd seen Heinz come and go by foot during the past thirty-six hours. The night before, he'd seen Miss Porter arrive in her old Ford. "I'm afraid she didn't leave until early morning." I wasn't too happy hearing that, and I could tell Roth didn't like it much either, even though he referred to it as "all standard stuff."

After he polished off the pie, Roth said he had to check back in at home because one of his daughters was sick. "How'd you like to take over for a couple of hours? You can stay right here. I'll take the Packard back at the station."

Having convinced my mother that I had a study date and might be home late, I was free and clear. The idea of staking out by myself was thrilling.

"Now all I want you to do is take notes," Roth instructed. "You know . . . names, times, etcetera. And don't leave the car. If you can't see everything from here, don't worry. Just get what you can." When he left, Roth reminded me once again to be patient. I was beginning to hate that word.

Before long I'd become lonely and cold. With my eyes fixed on Heinz's house, I found the blanket behind the seat and wrapped it around me. I thought about what I'd do if I had my own gun, something to shove under Big Lew's nose to give him the fright of his life. I wanted to be the hero, the guy who nailed Big Lew. Not just for the glory, but for Buddy.

Earlier, I had called Buddy's nurse only to learn that there was "no change." I was well aware that even if Buddy did come out of his coma, the doctors had serious doubts about his ever walking again. So that afternoon I made a special prayer for him at the temple. Slowly but surely I was beginning to get a grasp of God and religion, and their place in my life.

After an hour or so of battling with the prickly blanket, my breathing became slower and I fought the urge to close my eyes. Then someone emerged from the house. It was Big Lew's mother, who was carrying what appeared to be a filled shopping net. Pausing at the curb, she looked up and down the street before setting off. No matter what Roth had instructed, I couldn't resist slipping out of the car to tail her. Patience was never my strong suit.

I followed at least fifty feet behind, changing pace, trying to look casual. After a few blocks she turned right on Maple and paused again to look around. I tried to throw her off by pretending I was entering a nearby house. As I opened the gate and stepped into the dark yard, there was a dog's growl and I could make out a pair of yellow eyes about waist high, intently fixed on mine. Backing away, I snapped the gate shut and raced down the street looking for Mrs. Heinz, the dog barking all the while behind me. Thinking I'd lost her, I started back for the car until I spotted her going into a house on the corner of Maple and Ash. I moved closer to read the number in the dim light: 135 Maple. Quickly I crossed the road and disappeared into the shadows. A light popped on inside the house just as some older kids, with skates slung over their shoulders, approached.

At around 10:15, I checked my watch and remembered I said I'd be home at 9:30. Two things were painfully clear: not only were my parents going to be suspicious, but I could just see Roth's face when he found out I hadn't been patient.

∿

"I thought you said you had a study date," my mother remarked as I raided the fridge; I'd sneaked in through the store and then up into the kitchen, hoping to make it to my room undetected. But my mother had the ears of a wolf.

"I did have a study date."

"Well, when it got to be ten o'clock, I called the LaBeck house."

I continued searching for a snack, but realized the jig was up. "Actually, I didn't go right to Evette's. I stopped at the hospital first."

Whenever I lied my ears used to redden—a quirk my body had never outgrown. And of all the people who could read this, my mother was most skilled. She didn't say anything for awhile but I could tell she was merely waiting to see where I was going to take my improvised story.

"Buddy's still in a coma you know, and I was trying to see if he could hear me." I hated lying about that. "Before I knew it, it was ten o'clock."

Then, just as I thought I'd conned her, she said, "You were with Lieutenant Roth, weren't you, Zachary. I promised your father . . ."

I wondered what color my ears were now. "I know. And he's talked to me," I said, pouring myself a glass of watery milk. "Any bread?"

"In the breadbox. Peanut butter's in the cupboard." She gave me a resigned but warm look. "You know, your father's right. We discussed it at great length. And even though I have the greatest trust and respect for Lieutenant Roth, this is a murder case. So I'm backing your father one hundred per cent."

"Reva?" my father called from their bedroom.

"I'll be right there!" Before leaving, my mother turned to me. "I'm not going to nag any more, Zachary. All I ask is that you use good judgment. And let what happened to Buddy be a warning to you." She paused for dramatic effect. "Promising you'll be careful is not always enough. Promises are too easily broken, like bones. Remember that."

Using Buddy as an example proved more effective than if she'd yelled at me. I gulped in understanding. Her strategy was smart and sound, the kind you only appreciate years later.

As I sat down to read the comics with my milk and peanut butter sandwich, it suddenly became clear that when America had gone off to war, so too did the funny-paper characters. Smilin' Jack had joined the Army Air Force. Terry fought Japs instead of Pirates and while Daddy Warbucks served as a General, Little Orphan Annie collected scrap metal. For some reason, Dick Tracy and Li'l Abner avoided the service. But the funnies weren't as funny in war.

When the war ended, the cartoon characters were forced to adjust back to civilian life like everyone else and the strips regained some of their humor. Unfortunately for me, their timing was bad. I had lost my sense of humor completely.

24

School without Buddy just wasn't the same. I had learned the hard way how much he really meant to me. Even though we hadn't spent a lot of time together the past few weeks, knowing that Buddy wasn't there to clown around with was dismaying. Popovich and Birdwell were hardly what I considered fun to be with—neither had any interest in sports or criminology, not to mention girls. Popovich probably had little interest in anything, except maybe some miracle cure for acne.

The only bright spot left in my life was art class with Miss Porter. But that didn't begin until 1:15 each day after I'd already waded though the muck of Algebra and Latin. At least Miss Porter gave me something to look forward to.

At lunch time I shared my chicken sandwich with Melissa, who looked especially pretty in her white angora sweater and pleated pink skirt. Although mismatching socks were in style, I didn't like the way they looked on her. "You really think they look good?"

She glanced down at her socks, one blue and one pink. "Sure. All the kids are wearing them."

"I think they look dopey."

"Why are you so grumpy, Zachary?"

"Maybe because my best friend is in the hospital," I snapped back.

"Sorry, Zack. I miss him, too. It's funny how when somebody's gone, you like them more than when they were around. You know what I mean?"

I was the only one in our family who got on with Melissa. She was always too shy to say anything to my mother and father, who were convinced she couldn't talk until at age ten she tripped down the back stairs and swore like hell for nearly five minutes. And Melissa ignored Lenny. After he'd said her dream crooner was so skinny, citing that you couldn't tell "which was Sinatra and which was the microphone," Melissa stopped speaking to Lenny altogether.

Because there was no Hebrew school that day, I was expecting a confrontation with Roth. So I devised a way to avoid him and get back to Maple Street for some investigating on my own. I used a trick I had perfected in the fifth grade to elude Carl Judd and his "steel fists," as he called them. At exactly 2:55 I would ask to go to the Boys' Room. Then, grabbing my stuff from my locker in the hallway, I'd slip out of school from the Girls' Entrance. Luckily, I fooled Roth too. I was in no mood for another lecture on patience.

As I passed Smith's Pond some kids were playing hockey. They looked like they didn't have a worry in the world. It seemed so unfair. I couldn't understand why I had so many problems. But standing there watching the kids zigzagging across the ice, it dawned on me that Buddy might never skate again. For a moment I wished that it could have been one of *them* who got hit, not my best friend. But that wasn't fair either. Considering how I felt, it might as well have been me knocked out in that hospital bed. At least there would've been no pain, no confusion. As I cried, the tears made tiny holes in the snow at my feet.

◦✗

I must have been standing at the pond's edge for twenty minutes when the whistle at Keller Plastic blew long and loud, marking the end of the day shift. I figured there was still enough time to stop at St. Luke's for a visit with Buddy after a quick investigation.

Approaching 135 Maple Street cautiously and quietly, I could see that the place was terribly run down: dirty brown shingles, junk, and dead branches littered the yard. As a matter of fact, the entire neighborhood looked somewhat seedy. I paused in the shadows to study the house and determined it was unoccupied. So I made my way to the back yard, hunched behind an old concrete incinerator and waited some more. I didn't want to make any mistakes, not here.

I don't know exactly what possessed me, other than a strange sense of invincibility, but I opened my Tom Mix Ranger Knife and approached one of the back windows. I suppose I reasoned that God wouldn't let anything happen to me after what he'd put Buddy through. My adrenalin was flowing, but curiously I don't remember being even the slightest bit scared. I also believed I was operating in the name of the law, minus the badge and a .38, of course.

Except for the dog barking in the distance, it was quiet. The only other time I'd broken into a home was when Buddy had been locked out of his house and we jimmied the window in the laundry room to get in. But breaking in was fairly easy.

Once inside, I closed the window, made my way into the kitchen and looked around. On the counter next to the sink was a platter with two withered apples. I opened the refrigerator, which contained a couple of bottles of beer, a half-filled jar of mustard and a few graying sausages. In the vegetable bin below, I found an old cabbage and some spuds.

There was hardly any furniture about. And the master bedroom contained only a single bed, neatly made. Opening the closet, I found the rack half-filled with a man's clothing. On the floor was a pair of fairly new slippers and some worn, leather riding boots. I'd always wanted boots, but my folks considered them much too militaristic for a "nice Jewish boy."

I examined one of the suits, which was brown and scratchy. The label inside the jacket was from a cheap department store in Waterbury. In the dark corner of the closet there was a canvas suitcase. I placed it on the bed and opened it without hesitation. Something was driving me along, something capable of overriding all those instincts of fear that usually keep young boys out of trouble. Not this time.

Inside, I found a full-length, wool, blue-grey coat with no buttons. It resembled the coat Birdwell's uncle had brought back from the war as a memento. Birdwell had worn it, along with a German helmet, to school one day; not unexpectedly, he was greeted by a full day of snickers and jeers.

I folded the coat as I found it, then closed the suitcase and put it back. Searching through the dresser drawers, I found a faded snapshot of two tow-headed kids in short pants. I also turned up a pillbox wrapped in a clean handkerchief. Three tiny white tablets rolled around inside. I slipped one into my pocket.

Then the sound of laughter outside stiffened my legs. Peeking out the window from behind a dusty shade, I spotted a few men, probably from the factory, heading up the street.

I returned to the window I'd entered, and hurried back out. But in my haste I tore my shirt sleeve on the broken latch and scraped my forearm. The voices outside had grown much closer so I jumped to the ground and ran, hopping through scraggy bushes and over the fence that bordered the yard. Safely away from the house, I made my way across a rocky field, then hustled back towards the lakeshore.

The kids who were skating earlier had all gone home. The frozen pond was quiet and calm. But my heart was racing with terrified excitement. It had gone exactly as I planned: in like a snake, out like a fox. The only problem was my arm, which began to throb with searing pain as I reached our apartment.

25

On my way to visit Buddy, I spotted the Chevy stake-out car parked across from Heinz's place. Roth was camped in the front seat just staring straight ahead. I considered ducking out of sight to avoid a lecture, but I realized that sooner or later he would catch up with me. As I approached, Roth's head turned and he glared at me.

"I know you're mad," I said. "But I figured the smart thing was to follow anyone who left the house."

"Well, you figured wrong," Roth said, gesturing me into the car. I opened the passenger side door, climbed in and sat there silently. Roth took a deep breath, just like my father did when he was upset. "Look, when I told you not to leave the car, I meant it." His tone was considerably more stern than my father's. "This is no kid's game of cops and robbers, dammit!"

"Well I'm *no kid!*" I shot back. "And I don't play cops and robbers anymore." The words spilled out faster than I could manage. "If you arrested Big Lew when I told you I was the witness, this entire case would've been over already." Then I iced the cake: "And Buddy probably never would've gotten hurt."

Roth whirled around. "Listen," he said. "Don't you ever tell me how to do my job!"

I scrunched down in my seat under the weight of his fury.

"I've already told you," he continued, his anger slowly diffusing. "We've got a chance to grab a high-ranking Nazi officer right here in Oakville. I can't tell you how important that could be."

"But we've got more than enough to nail Big Lew, *and* this stupid officer guy."

"We don't have crap on the Nazi," Roth said. "We don't even know who he *is.*"

It was time to play my trump card. "Maybe you don't, but I do," I said. Roth's eyes demanded an explanation. "I, uh, did some investigating on my own after I gave you the slip."

The way Roth chewed his lip, I figured I shouldn't have mentioned anything about dodging him after school. Regardless, he remained silent as I told him exactly how I had followed Mrs. Heinz and broken into 135 Maple Street. "I used my Ranger Knife to pry open the window." I could tell he was intrigued by what I had to say, so I continued, describing everything I'd seen: the coat, pillbox, the boots, even the refrigerator contents. "Now we can nail him, right?"

Roth spoke to me calmly. "First of all, Zack, you can't break into a man's house without a search warrant. And you certainly can't arrest somebody on evidence obtained from an illegal break-in. You've got to do things in a sane and civilized way," he said. "Don't you understand? That's one of the reasons we fought the war."

"The Nazis didn't fight fair, so why do we have to be civilized with them?"

"Because we don't want to lower ourselves to their level."

I was confused.

"Once again, all this is going to take patience," he said. "It's as simple as that."

"It's kinda hard to be sane and civilized when you're best pal is in a coma."

At first, Roth didn't respond, and we sat silently as I fidgeted with the glovebox latch.

"Over six million Jews were annihilated by the Nazis during World War II," Roth said. "Six million people destroyed." He paused. "It makes me sick to think about that number and all those souls. My mind just can't accept it." His voice quivered. "And one of those people was my father. That's what really hurts." Roth sighed. "Jacob Rothstein. That was our name, Rothstein. Forget that my father was one of the great Jewish scholars and intellectuals of Vilna. He was loving and caring. And he made the world a better place."

"Why did you change your name?" I asked.

"My father thought it would be safer when he sent us off to America And that's why I want this Nazi so bad," he continued with growing passion. "Heinz is just another small town crook who'll get his due in the end. But to catch a Nazi. To catch one of the men responsible for decimating all those people. That's what I'm after. But it has to be done right." I watched the fury in Roth building. "Of course I've considered what I'll do when I catch him. I even thought about throttling the bastard. It's tempting, believe me." His fingers were clenched into a tight fist. "I can only pray for the strength to remain civilized."

"Six million. Jeez."

"It's absolutely incredible," Roth said. "And the aftermath in Europe is driving the survivors to one of

two extremes. Either there's a flight from Judaism,"
he explained, "or an intensification of Jewishness."

"Yeah, my father told me about all those Jews
trying to find a new home."

"Exactly," Roth nodded. "Palestine. They want to
establish their own new identity in Palestine. Somewhere away from the land where their families were
slaughtered."

It was difficult to identify with the plight of European Jews. I was still trying to come to terms with my
own Jewishness, let alone the rest of the Hebrews.
But the one thing that really moved me was Roth
losing his father to the Nazis.

✧

My mother made potato pancakes for dinner—her
specialty. Lenny and my father had shared their meal
earlier, after which my father retreated to the store
while Lenny listened to "Mr. and Mrs. North" in the
living room. As I devoured dinner, my mother hovered over me like a hawk.

"I never see you with Melissa anymore," she com-
mented, with what seemed like satisfaction. "What's
the matter?"

It was amazing how much my mother knew about
my private life. "I've been really busy with other
stuff," I said.

"I just hope your schoolwork isn't suffering."

"No, no." Actually, I was teetering on the brink of
failing two courses.

"Candy Keller's birthday is this weekend," she said. "I think she's having a party."

"Good for her." I got up from the table as Lenny called in from the living room, "Wanna play Monopoly, Zack?"

"No. I've gotta do my algebra!" My mother smiled, pleased. The truth of the matter was, Algebra was more appealing than playing Monopoly with Lenny, who the last time we played, bought Park Place and Boardwalk on his first trip around the board and had hotels all over the place in no time. I made the mistake of calling him a cheater and suffered the consequences—Lenny was highly skilled in tweaking my ear.

After doing the dishes, I escaped to my room and closed the door. Because I'd left the window open it was almost freezing inside. Searching through a couple of drawers for my old pair of longjohns, I came across my Jack Armstrong paraphernalia and carefully laid the gizmos out on my bed. Curiously, the thrill was gone; the special gadgets no longer held the fascination for me they once did. I suppose reality had supplanted fantasy in my life. No longer was I forced to imagine adventure and mystery. Instead, I found myself imagining a simpler existence. What I would've given to have ol' Oakville back.

Mentally exhausted, I lay down with my algebra book in hand. Had my mother came in she would probably have fainted dead away. But there was a method to my madness. Algebra had always been a pleasant way of putting me right to sleep.

Before I knew it, I was seated at an ebony grand piano, barefooted, wearing a sharp-looking, white tuxedo. I was playing "Till The End of Time," currently number one on "Your Hit Parade," when from behind a marble column, Miss Porter appeared in a pink garter belt, with long, rose-colored nylon stockings and nothing else. She settled down beside me and placed her warm hands over mine.

"Shhhh," she whispered, placing a finger on her shiny lips. "Silence is golden."

I couldn't agree more. Inhaling deeply, I began nuzzling her soft, warm neck. And her sweet, flowery fragrance lulled my senses.

26

Anxious to spend some time with Buddy before school, I hustled down to St. Luke's at 7 A.M. My secret hope was that I might be the one to pull him out of the darkness, the way he had done for me at Black Rock. I saw it as my chance to pay back my best pal and even the score.

In the hospital room, Buddy was still lying there, unchanged. The tubes going in and out of his nose and mouth had been removed, but his head was fully bandaged. His arm was in a cast and he was still being fed intravenously. He looked peaceful enough, but I got the impression that no one was holding their breath for him to come around.

The room was wall-to-wall with "Get Well" cards and flowers, and I knew how thrilled Buddy would've been to see them, as he never received much in the way of gifts from his parents. Buddy used to get the biggest kick over a simple birthday card.

With half an hour before school, I sat at Buddy's bedside and opened my Latin book. As far as I was concerned, Latin was as boring as the people who spoke it. Who gave a grape how many legions Octavius commanded? It was ridiculous. So, figuring Buddy would appreciate hearing me struggle through my lesson, I talked myself through the first exercise aloud. After a few moments, there was another voice in the room.

"Melissa . . ."

Holding my breath, I turned my head slowly and studied Buddy's face.

"Melissa . . ."

Buddy's eyes were closed. But his body seemed to be stirring, twisting slightly.

"Melissa?" His eyes blinked open, squinting. And he coughed, gaining consciousness.

My first thought was that my prayers had been answered. But my second thought was that Buddy had come out of the whole thing retarded, the coma somehow scrambling his brains. Racing out into the corridor, I shouted for help. Within seconds, a nurse rushed from another room, dropped the tray of food in her hands and followed me back into the room. She immediately gave Buddy a sip of water then jammed a thermometer into his mouth.

"Thank God," she murmured.

"Yeah, thank God." I moved closer, but Buddy still didn't seem to recognize me. He was sort of grinning, but his expression was glazed and dull. "I'd better call the Goodsons," I said, hurrying towards the lobby phone.

"I'll call Dr. Reade at home," the nurse said.

After I hung up from talking to Claire, I puzzled again over why Buddy had mumbled Melissa's name and not mine. It didn't make sense.

oℐʳ

When I happily announced to the class that Buddy had regained consciousness, I watched carefully as

Melissa whooped and hollered along with all the other kids. Or did she whoop and holler louder than the other kids? I could only reason that my mind was playing tricks on me. Or maybe Buddy's mind was playing tricks on him. I shouldn't have cared whose name he spoke: mine, Melissa's or Minnie Mouse's. He was out of the clouds and back on earth. I should've been eternally grateful. And I was, but there was something wrong.

All during history I couldn't take my eyes off Melissa. She was wearing that pretty angora sweater I liked so much. My mind started weaving lewd visions of her and Buddy together, naked and passionate. After mentally backtracking, I decided that their romance must have flowered while I had been busy with Roth all those afternoons. Of course, I still clung to the hope that Buddy might just have been delirious.

"Zachary!" the teacher suddenly called out. "Can you tell us who invented the printing press?"

I hauled myself up from the desk and racked my overloaded brain. I knew it was some German, but the only name in my mind was Melissa. "Sorry," I mumbled.

As I slunk down, Melissa glanced back with an "any-jerk-knows-that" frown. Instinctively, I buried my face in my book. Everything had seemed fine sharing that chicken sandwich. But then again, I realized I might have made Melissa angry when I cracked about her socks. Then I remembered that Buddy actually liked Sinatra and it all started adding up: Buddy likes bobbysox, Melissa likes Sinatra and bobbysox— Melissa loves Buddy, and he loves Melissa.

Suddenly I heard Birdwell call out: "That's easy. Gutenberg invented the printing press!"

That little creep just had to preface every answer with "That's easy!"

"That's right, Alan," the teacher beamed. "Did you hear that, Zachary?"

"Yeah, Gutenbird," I mumbled, barely raising from the depths of my book.

"Gutenberg, dummy!" Birdwell corrected.

The whole class laughed heartily at my expense.

After school, I hurried home to ask my mother a big favor. Realizing how much Buddy's recovery meant to me, she allowed me to skip Hebrew school again. This time so I could visit with my friend at the hospital. Sprinting all the way there, I was winded when I arrived.

We looked each other over for a few silent seconds. Buddy noticed me breathing hard. "Outta shape again, huh?"

"Again? Hell, I'll whip you easy in some one-on-one just as soon as you get out of here."

He didn't reply. Instead, his eyes welled and he glanced at the nurse, who had been adjusting his i.v. setup.

"What's wrong?" I asked.

The nurse looked at me, then back at Buddy. Finally, she turned away and left the room without a word. Tears started streaming down Buddy's face, which was turned away from me.

After an awkward minute, I said, "I'll be right back," then left the room. The nurse was at her desk, writing on a chart. "What's going on?"

She didn't even look up as she continued with her

report. "Buddy might be paralyzed," she said, avoiding my eyes. "He can't move his legs. But nothing's certain." Her voice was soft and strained. "We had a neurologist in from Waterbury," she continued. "And we're going to run a lot of tests." Her words weren't making it to my ears anymore. She said something about Buddy's "central nervous system," but I was feeling dizzy and having trouble getting enough air into my lungs.

Running down the corridor towards the main entrance, I banged open the restroom door with my shoulder and doubled over, sobbing. "IT'S NOT FAIR!" I screamed. "It's not fair!" My voice echoed. "Why'd it have to be Buddy? WHY?" I hoped God could hear me because I wanted an answer. But I didn't get one. Finally, holding my head, I was able to stop the tears, and my hurt turned to anger. Looking up, I said: "I prayed, dammit."

27

Later that week after glee club rehearsal, I finagled a few moments alone with Miss Porter by asking if I could help collect the sheet music. We had just started practicing for the annual Christmas Show and she seemed to welcome my assistance.

"We're going to miss Buddy," she said. "He was a terrific tenor."

"He's not dead, you know."

She flushed with embarrassment. "I'm sorry, Zachary. I didn't mean it like that."

"I'll bet he even makes it to the party this year."

"I really hope so."

I couldn't take my eyes off her perfect, creamy complexion. It might have been the soft afternoon light, but I couldn't spot a single blemish. Even in my dreams I never imagined Miss Porter prettier or sexier than she was at that moment. She caught me staring, but thankfully didn't comment. This only fueled my fire.

"I had a dream about you last night."

"Really?" she said coyly. "Tell me about it."

Obviously I couldn't tell her everything, but I did describe the ebony piano and how I played "Till The End of Time."

"Oh yes, that's from a classical piece," she said. "Chopin's Polonaise in A-flat." She sat down at the piano. I slipped right beside her without an invitation. "Opus 53," she added.

I reveled in the lilac aura which surrounded her, and slowly began to perspire as I studied her hands. Miss Porter's piano rendition had so much more feeling than the recording I'd heard so often.

When she finished, I gulped and said, "That was swell." Certainly not my favorite expression, it felt right, nonetheless, as she blushed.

She suddenly gathered her things, breaking the spell. "Have you been thinking about cello lessons, Zachary?"

"Actually, basketball's been taking up most of my spare time." A fabrication, but I yearned for Miss Porter to envision me as an athlete.

"Well, I'm not going to give up on you," she said. "I've said it before and I'll say it again. You have a special talent for art and music, Zachary."

It was my turn to blush.

"And you really mustn't think it's sissy stuff," she said. "Did you know that George Gershwin was a weightlifter?"

"I don't really know much about Gershwin," I said, eager to change the subject. "So, Lieutenant Roth told me he talked to you."

"He did?" She grinned. "You two working together now?"

"Kinda," I said. "So, what do you think of him?"

"He seems like a marvelous detective," she said. "I really find his line of work fascinating. I wish I knew more about him."

It occurred to me that bringing up the subject of Roth was not the smartest move.

"He's so intelligent and sensitive," she said. "A real breath of fresh air." She glanced out the window, then turned back, looking worried, as if Big Lew was waiting outside.

"Yeah, the lieutenant's a pretty good guy." I tried to sound nonchalant. "I'm glad I can help him out sometimes."

Then she became serious and gazed directly into my eyes. "Zachary, I want you to be very careful. Please, promise me that."

My stomach fluttered. "What do you mean?"

"Now I'm just guessing, but whoever was responsible for Buddy's accident was probably trying to keep him quiet," she said. "But with him still alive and with you being his best friend, there's the chance that he might tell you everything, or so some people may think."

That she thought Buddy's accident was an attempt to silence him concerned me. The word around town was that some drunk had run him down. Of course, Roth and I had other ideas, but I assumed it was something he would never share with Miss Porter.

At that point, I was tempted to tell her that I was the one who had seen everything and that poor Buddy was the wrong guy to go after. But I stopped myself, knowing that the truth would all be out soon enough. Still, I had this feeling that in the end, Miss Porter might resent me for not leveling with her from the beginning. But how could I be sure she was being honest with me?

"Thanks for the help," she said, touching my shoulder lightly with her hand.

"Any time."

I watched her leave, then went to the window. As I suspected, Big Lew was out there, leaning smugly against her car.

⌇

I needed some time alone to think things over, so I headed for Olaf's Auto Body to shoot some buckets. There were a few half-frozen puddles in the playing area, but that didn't bother me as I was used to playing outdoor basketball in all sorts of weather.

I tried a hook shot and sank it easily. This brought a slight smile to my face as I recalled teaching Buddy that shot, and how it quickly became his favorite. The problem was, he could never sink it in our one-on-ones. He had to be stationary, concentrating, with his tongue peeking out of the corner of his mouth.

I tried another one. Swish. But my smile had disappeared. The possibility of never playing with Buddy again was looming large.

"Can I shoot with ya, Zack?"

I turned, startled by the raspy voice. It was Porky Olaf, the half-witted son of Gus Olaf. Porky wasn't ornery like his father. He was fat and dull, but well-liked by almost everybody. He was like a big, friendly dog who always wanted to play fetch.

Porky's father, on the other hand, was detested in Oakville. He wore the same cruddy T-shirt and filthy overalls all year round. Known as the shady operator and owner of Olaf's Auto Body, Gus kept strictly to himself, regularly drinking heavily and cussing out Porky.

I really wanted to play alone but didn't have the heart to tell Porky that. "Okay . . . let's play." I flipped him the ball.

Porky took a shot that slammed hard against the rim and deflected over to the parked cars alongside the paint shop. "I'll get it," he said, scurrying to retrieve it.

I watched as he squirmed under a wrecked Dodge until all that could be seen of him was his chunky butt and squatty legs. Finally he wriggled and kicked until he came up grinning with the ball. "Catch!" he shouted, all enthused.

We had hardly started and already Porky was having the time of his life. "Listen to this. I got the day off," he said. "My ol' man's working in the shop at the junkyard and told me to get lost. Lucky, huh?"

I nodded and dribbled out past the foul line. Throughout World War II, Gus Olaf had collected junk. And I recalled how he got all the Oakville kids thinking they were contributing to the war effort by putting up signs saying: "One useless old tire can provide enough rubber for twelve gas masks," or, "One old radiator has enough steel for seventeen .30 caliber rifles." My personal favorite was, "One beat-up washing machine can make six 75 millimeter mortar shells." All of us pitched in to collect junk for free, then handed it over to Gus, who turned around and sold it to the government for a tidy profit.

"Listen to this. My ol' man's fixin' Big Lew's coupe and don't want no distractions," Porky announced.

"Really?" I paused, waiting for him to continue.

"Well, Big Lew brought that coupe of his in last week, said he hit a deer drivin' one night." Porky told the story slowly, constructing his sentences one word at a time. I knew that even if I didn't pump him,

Porky would blab everything sooner or later. "My ol' man said he'd get right on it. But listen to this. Big Lew told him to tow it over to the junkyard and work on it there." Porky was trying to dribble as he spoke, but only splashed muddy water on his already crusty pant legs.

I couldn't resist a little prod. "You see the dent, Pork?"

"Uh huh," he nodded. "Right fender was all bashed in. Poor fuckin' deer."

Poor fuckin' Buddy, I thought.

"Listen to this. My ol' man wanted to give the coupe a new color job, maybe maroon or somethin'. But Big Lew wants it just like it was."

I shook my head, trying to remain calm.

"Well, that ain't nothin'," Porky giggled. "I found this in back of the car." No doubt this was the highlight of Porky's story. "It was bigger, but I tore it to fit my pocket," he added.

He handed over to me what was once a pinup shot featuring a smiling lady with huge knockers in a one-piece bathing suit. I grinned, then told Porky I wasn't feeling so hot and handed back the picture. "I better get going, Pork."

He folded the picture back up and beamed. "Thanks a heap for the game, Zack," he said, then wandered off humming.

28

As soon as I got home I called Roth in Waterbury. An elderly-sounding lady with a Yiddish accent answered, and I could hear Roth's twins squabbling in the background. The woman told me that as it was Friday, Harry was at the synagogue saying Kaddish. I'd heard about Kaddish before, but I didn't know exactly what it meant. Anyway, I didn't want Roth calling back, so I told her there was no message and that I'd see him later. After hanging up, I wandered into the kitchen and witnessed something I thought I'd never see: Maibaum, eyes tear-filled, was seated at the table clacking two empty beer bottles. He'd been slurping what must have been his third brew when he spotted me and went ghost white.

"Oh God, I hope you don't tell your family about this," Maibaum said, forcing a cockeyed smile.

Lucky for him, my mother and father had gone to a movie and Lenny was still at the bowling alley; they would've embarrassed Maibaum with a thousand questions, my father no doubt spearheading the investigation.

"Don't worry," I said. "Loose Lips Sink Ships." Opening the fridge, I was relieved to discover that at least Maibaum hadn't been at the milk. "So what's the problem, Dave?"

"Funny you should ask," Maibaum said, taking another swig of beer. I helped myself to some peanut butter and Wonder Bread and sat down, hoping he would start babbling.

"I bet you think I'm getting tanked because they're gonna let me go at Keller Plastic," he said. "But that's only half of it, Zack."

I looked at him, recalling how he'd always been so proper and in control of himself. "Damn Keller," Maibaum ranted, "Ruined everything when he hired that new bastard."

If my father had seen him in that state, he surely would've sent Dave packing. Not that I wouldn't have approved, but I hated to see anyone kicked while they were down—even if it was "The Baum."

"Did I ever tell you about my mother, Zack?" Before I could even shake my head, he continued. "She's a W-WAC," he said. "A f-full . . . g-goddamn c-colonel."

"That's great, Dave." I smiled uneasily, imagining his mother in full military dress, with khaki underwear no less.

Maibaum took what I hoped was his final slug of beer, polishing off the third bottle with a burp. "My father's only a corporal, you know."

That was news to me, too.

"You know how many more stripes a c-colonel's got over a corporal? You know how many, Zack?"

I shook my head.

"Let's just say a lot." More tears juiced from Maibaum's half-shut eyes as he belched. "Mama's asking for a divorce now. She wants to be a career soldier. A career goddamn soldier! Can you believe that?"

The image Maibaum had carefully constructed over the previous few months, that of a sober and brilliant chemical engineer, had suddenly crumbled before me.

"So what?" I tried to comfort him. "At least she's got a good job and gets to wear a cool uniform." I didn't know what else to say, but it seemed to help.

Maibaum grinned, then started to chuckle. "You're right." He set the empty bottle down and gave his nose a good blast. Then he tried to stand, but couldn't make it on his own. So I hauled him out of the chair and guided him to his room.

Once he was settled onto his bed, I asked, "How'd you like to tackle a secret assignment, Dave?" I'd been waiting for the right time to give him the little white pill for analysis.

Maibaum saluted. "I'd love it, sir." Then he flopped back onto his pillow. "First thing in the morning." He closed his eyes, and within moments, slipped off to sleep.

⁊

At breakfast, Lenny was showing off by singing "Chickery-chick." He didn't know all the words, but had latched onto: ". . . bol-li-ka wol-li-ka can't you see, Chickery-chick is me!" He kept repeating the phrase, singing it louder each time. Neither Maibaum, who had a terrible hangover, nor I, was impressed.

"By tomorrow, I'll know the whole song by heart," Lenny boasted.

"Wow," I said sarcastically. "Can I have your autograph?"

Our parents were already out and about, so no one in authority was around to police the battle that erupted. Lenny grabbed a ballpoint from his pocket, wrestled me to the linoleum and scrawled his name across my forehead. All the while, I was hollering for him to stop.

"Please," Maibaum pleaded. "Keep it down!" He pinched his temples. "My head . . ."

Finally, I struggled up and tried to wipe the marks from my face. I always hated being strong-armed by Lenny. "I bet you didn't know 'Till the End of Time' was from 'The Polonaise' by Chopin," I bragged.

"Yeah," Lenny smirked. "And I bet you didn't know buffalo shit's green! Who cares!?"

Maibaum winced and excused himself from the table.

"Hey Dave!" I called. "Remember what I asked last night?"

Lenny looked at us, puzzled. "What about last night?"

"Nothing. It's personal business between me and Dave."

"Oh . . . Zacky doin' business with 'The Baum' now?" Lenny teased.

Escorting Maibaum out of the kitchen and into his room, I locked the door and presented him with the tablet. Then I asked him to analyze it at the factory lab and report back to me a.s.a.p. "Don't forget, this is top secret," I added, giving him a mock salute.

"Right," Maibaum said, carefully placing the pill in his clean pocket handkerchief. He forced a grin, half-heartedly returned the salute, then left for work.

Before leaving for class, I called St. Luke's and told Buddy I'd come by as soon as I returned from Hebrew school. "And save me something good to eat," I said, knowing he hadn't finished one hospital meal since he'd been there.

"You can have my Jell-O," Buddy said.

Since Buddy hated Jell-O, I wasn't sure if that was a friendly gesture or if he was trying to stick it to me, like old times. Either way, I was glad as hell to have Buddy back.

29

On the bus ride back from Hebrew school I was lucky enough to land a window seat. Everyone outside was bundled up and bucking the wind as they trampled through patches of filthy, crusted snow—the chief side-effect of winter. I spotted a couple of kids with hockey sticks and skates, and it dawned on me that I hadn't had time to play once since Smith's Pond had frozen over. It seemed like all I had time for now was watching other kids having fun. Ideally, I would've gotten my hoped-for basketball career back on track and straightened out my love life. But as soon as I got off the bus, Roth flagged me down from the Packard.

"Any news?" he inquired anxiously.

I quickly briefed him about the dented coupe. But he wanted to see it for himself. So we headed for the junkyard immediately.

"I'll bet you didn't know that Olaf's Junk is exactly two-and-a-half miles from my house."

Roth glanced over at me. "Is that something I'm *supposed* to know?"

"Not if you don't have a Jack Armstrong Pedometer."

He smiled. "A what?"

"A pedometer," I said, pulling the gadget from my pocket. "Measures distances when you walk," I explained. "Works great. I just set it for my normal stride, which is 25 inches. And it tells exactly how far I walk."

"Sounds pretty handy."

"Personally, I think every good detective should have one. And I've got a Frank Buck Explorer's Sun Watch with a built-in compass."

"Wouldn't that be something if we solved this case with toys," Roth mused.

I didn't care much for his sarcasm. "You never know."

"That's right. You never know."

As we accelerated to make it through a yellow light, Roth grinned uneasily, then cleared his throat. "Uh, did I tell you I got a call from Wentworth?"

"Nope."

"He said he's promised Heinz's defense lawyer to stop any further investigation one week before the trial."

"Why?"

"Obviously he's sympathetic to Big Lew."

"What happens if we can't nail this thing down by then?"

Roth chewed his lip, and we continued towards Olaf's Junk. "Well, we've got your testimony. The rest'll come, you'll see." He peered over at me. "Remember . . . patience."

The sun was disappearing behind the trees as we turned onto the dirt road leading to the junkyard. Wrecked cars and trucks were scattered along the roadside, debris everywhere. We slowed to a stop at the high chain-link fence surrounding Olaf's Junk, got out of the car and looked around. The place was bleak and deserted, made doubly ominous by the onset of darkness. A battered sign wired to the fence read: UNLESS YOU'RE LOOKING FOR TROUBLE—SCRAM!

The yard was ugly with patches of oil-blackened snow. Since the gate was half open, Roth suggested we check out the yard. Reluctantly, I agreed. Inside, there was dog crap all over and urine stains in the snow, but no one was in sight, man or animal. Roth warned me to stick close as we moved through the piled wreckage towards a decrepit garage.

It was ghostly quiet except for the wind that hummed through the abandoned junk. I almost grabbed onto Roth's jacket for support, but I was consciously trying to hold my own. Then suddenly, without warning, a huge dog sprang from the roof of a wrecked pickup onto Roth, sending him to the ground. It was a snarling Rottweiler.

The dog's jaws locked around Roth's arm, and the two rolled furiously around in the slush. The sounds were awful—Roth screaming, the beast snapping and barking. I cursed at the dog to stop, but it wouldn't. So, grabbing a rusty piece of bumper, I swung it overhead and brought it down with all my might, catching the frenzied animal square on the back of the neck. It let go, but didn't run. Instead, it growled and hunched for attack. So I took another swing and cracked him on the snout—which sent him whimpering off.

Roth was still in the muck, holding his arm and groaning. The Rottweiler had bitten through his coat sleeve and blood was seeping from the wound. Before I could say anything, Roth struggled to his feet. "I'm all right," he said. "Thanks for the help, pal."

"What if he comes back?"

"Dogs aren't that stupid," Roth said, clutching his arm.

"You never know."

"Maybe you're right. Let's just locate the coupe, then get the hell out of here."

Cautiously, we entered the old shop and looked around. There, among the cars ready for spraypainting, was the Olds. The front right bumper had been repaired and primed, the right headlight masked off. Roth checked the license plate, crouched to examine the bumper, then straightened, wincing and chomping his lower lip.

I noticed several drops of blood on the floor next to the wheel where he stood. It was obvious he was biting back the pain.

"I'll get my camera," Roth said. "It's in the car." Then he disappeared.

The moment had all the flavor of a real radio drama. It was like "The Adventures of Ellery Queen," with myself as young Ellery and Roth as the Inspector. But just as I started to enjoy the thrill of detective work, I was jolted by a sound, and whirled around. It was Big Lew.

"What's up, Silver?"

I could only gasp.

"I guess you didn't see that sign on the gate," he said.

Of course I saw it. You couldn't miss it. But I didn't say a word. I couldn't, and I wasn't about to admit anything even if I could. My eyes darted to Heinz's hands, expecting to spot a knife about to be plunged into my heart. But he held nothing. With his fists clenched, though, he took a small step forward.

I gulped and pictured myself in traction next to Buddy at St. Luke's. Where was Roth? Had the damn dog attacked him again? Or had he collapsed from loss of blood? My mind was swirling with anxious questions.

"How's Buddy?" Heinz asked.

I was still unable to talk.

"That was quite a nasty accident," he remarked, taking another step closer. Two more strides and he would've been standing on my toes. "If I was still running the department," he said, "I'd have already caught the fucker who banged your friend."

"But you aren't running the department," Roth's voice sounded from the shadows. "Are you?"

I sighed with relief.

The lieutenant stood coolly in the doorway behind Heinz, hand inside his coat pocket. I wasn't sure if Roth was clutching a .38 or cradling his wounded arm. Luckily, Big Lew wasn't sure either.

"You're breaking the law, Lieutenant," Heinz said. "This is private property."

"Then what are *you* doing here?" Roth said, "You're not the law anymore."

Big Lew, unblinking, kept his eyes glued on Roth. "If you were smart, Jewboy, you'd get the hell out of here." Neither Roth nor I budged. "Now!" Heinz added.

Roth grinned, then motioned with his head for me to skiddoo. So I took off without a glance backwards. When I made it out the gate, I jumped into the Packard and waited for my partner. A few moments later, Roth appeared and casually slid in behind the wheel. We started driving, but not nearly fast enough as far as I was concerned.

Roth couldn't hold back a smile. "Heinz knows how close we are to landing him," he said. "He's one scared sonofabitch."

That made two of us.

30

A fresh blanket of snow had fallen during the night, swaddling the town in brilliant white. So I dressed, bundling myself in my Mackinaw, and trudged out into the plush cold. Having been unable to visit Buddy the night before, I felt guilty, so I headed straight towards St. Luke's.

At the newsstand on Main Street, I bought the latest issue of *Sporting News* for Buddy, knowing I could always count on a hot argument with him about an article criticizing the Chicago Bears' defense. But when I opened the door to his hospital room, I found the bed empty.

A nurse, who'd noticed me enter, poked her head inside. "If you're looking for Buddy, he's down in X-ray."

I told her thanks and decided to wait. Taking off my coat, I settled onto the chair next to the bed, cracked open the paper and read about the great teamwork of Doc Blanchard and Glenn Davis in the recent Army-Notre Dame game at Yankee Stadium.

"Army's two backs are the best to come down the pike in years," the article stated. ". . . Blanchard, a human blockbuster, and Davis, a jet-propelled half-back, make their cream-smooth T-attack bubble and boil like no other T in the land. Once in the clear, Blanchard's beef-trust legs dance on eggshells. He has a 14-game average of 6.6 yards for every time he carries the ball. Davis, on the other hand, has a special kind of locomotion all his own . . ." I liked Davis best, because he was a player who piled up yardage on speed and skill, not power.

Pausing, I glanced around the room at all the cards and flowers and wondered if maybe the *Sporting News* might depress him, reading about all those athletes. So I folded the paper and stuffed it into my notebook. Without sports, however, I realized there was little for us to talk about.

I strolled around the room, checking out the floral arrangements, most of which had already wilted. Sifting through the cards, I came across an oversized one that caught my attention. It had a big red heart on the front. I opened it and read the inscription.

"Dear Boodles," it said. "My thoughts are with you day and night and I miss you very very much. Get well soon. Love, M.E."

Boodles? M.E.?

I heard squeaking and turned to see Buddy being wheeled into the room by an orderly. "How're you doin', Bud?"

He forced a smile. "Hiya, Zack." The orderly lifted him onto the bed and Buddy sighed, looking pale and exhausted.

After the orderly left, we gazed at each other for a long, awkward time without speaking. Something uncontrollable was boiling inside me.

"Boodles?" I blurted.

Buddy flushed as his eyes darted to the card with the big, red heart, which I was holding tight in my hands.

"Don't bend that, okay?" he said, indicating the card.

"Who's M.E.?" I said, setting it back on the table with the other cards. But I damn well knew the answer.

After a long pause, Buddy said, "Melissa Edwards. You know Melissa, don't you? She lives in the same building as you."

⌐✗

I was shattered about losing Melissa to Buddy. It felt like a whole year had passed without my knowing it, as if I was the one who had slipped into some deep sleep and awakened to find everything changed.

At school that day, Melissa was wearing her hair up like Miss Porter. She looked exceptionally pretty and mature—probably because she was no longer mine. And I started remembering the little questions Buddy had asked when he first discovered Melissa was my new neighbor. I also recalled the gleam in Melissa's eye when I introduced her to Buddy. Things were so clear, I wondered how I could've been so blind and stupid. Some detective I was; I couldn't even keep tabs on my girlfriend.

With Melissa gone, I turned my concern to the budding relationship between Roth and Miss Porter. I tried to cook up a plan to keep them apart, but before I realized it, the school bell sounded and everyone herded out.

As usual, Roth was standing next to the Packard, only now his arm was in a sling. "I got a tetanus shot at St. Luke's last night," he said.

"No stitches?"

"Didn't need any," Roth said. "By the way, I stopped in to see Buddy and he told me the guy driving the car wasn't Heinz."

"How could he tell?" The doctors explained to Mr. and Mrs. Goodson that first day at the hospital that Buddy was certain to suffer a memory lapse, which could result in substantial trauma. Otherwise, I would have asked him about the accident the moment he came around.

"Buddy said the second before he was struck, he caught a glimpse of the driver," Roth explained. "He said if it *was* Heinz, he'd have definitely recognized him."

"Yeah, but it was probably too dark." I wanted to see Big Lew take the rap for the hit and run on top of Greg Bondi's murder.

"I don't know. Buddy sounded very sure of himself," Roth said.

I explained to Roth what the doctors had said, but he did have a point. If Buddy had seen Big Lew driving, that was one thing he probably wouldn't have forgotten. "I can't do any more detective stuff tonight," I said. "My parents have just about had it with me coming home late for dinner."

"As a matter of fact," Roth said, "so has my wife."

All I could think was, "Wait 'til she gets a load of Miss Porter."

❧

As soon as I entered our apartment, Maibaum rushed up and demanded to speak with me privately.

I invited him to step into my "quarters," and shut the door. "Okay, what do you have?"

Maibaum looked around nervously, then confided, "I did an assay at the factory lab." He licked his lips. "It's c-c-cyanide." Whenever Maibaum got very excited, he stammered. "B-But it looks homemade, because the p-potassium isn't mixed in properly."

"So what does that mean?"

Maibaum kept rubbing his thumb and forefinger together nervously as he spoke. "It m-means that the p-pill was manufactured by an amateur." Maibaum continued, speaking faster now. "Did you know Goebbels gave c-cyanide to his six kids before shooting his w-wife and himself?" he said, "Heinrich Himmler and Field Marshall Ritter von Greim also took it in the final days." Bubbling with information, Maibaum was really enjoying himself. "All the Nazi big shots carried cyanide with them toward the end. There's rumors that some were even taught how to make it themselves from r-raw chemicals in c-case of emergency, and that looks like what you've got here." Removing his handkerchief to reveal the pill, Maibaum placed it in his palm for me to see.

I stared at the tablet, dumbfounded.

"Now where the hell did you get it?" Maibaum whispered.

I was not about to tell him, so I made up some story about a rat poison experiment for a science project at school. Maibaum squinted in disbelief. "Rat poison? This could kill an elephant!"

I tried to distract him. "At least you didn't get caught with it at the factory, or Keller really would've had good reason to fire you."

Maibaum winced, and the subject had been successfully changed. "D-Doesn't matter now anyway," he said. "The guy Keller hired seems to be working out just peachy. Supposedly, he's some kind of genius." Maibaum's head hung low. "With my luck, he'll be moving in on my job within the week."

"That bastard!" I said, still intent on keeping the subject off the cyanide pill.

This time Maibaum didn't mind the language, and nodded in agreement. "You'd think with my mother presenting Keller Plastic a Defense award, I could at least have counted on some job security." Maibaum continued, his irritation building as he jumped from conclusion to conclusion. "But I'm sure Keller's ready to fire ol' D-Dave Maibaum, who works right through his lunch break everyday. It's just not f-fair, dammit."

I carefully reclaimed the pill, thanked Maibaum for a job well done, then hurried him out of the room. Making a beeline for the telephone, I dialed Roth's home.

Roth's wife answered, and said he was out again. How could I sleep with news like that?

31

By the time lunch rolled around I was so anxious to tell the lieutenant the news about the cyanide pill that I couldn't enjoy my food—not that I was looking forward to a soggy meatloaf sandwich with no dessert. As soon as the final bell rang, I darted out ahead of the pack to find Roth leaning against "The Pack" with a pair of skates slung over his shoulder.

"How 'bout a little skating?" he said. "I thought we should live it up today."

Like a volcano erupting, I blurted: "The guy at 135 Maple's definitely a Nazi. He's got cyanide like all the other German officers."

"Interesting," Roth said, not responding as excitedly as I'd hoped. Climbing into the car I told him I needed to stop home to pick up my skates and hockey stick. "I had our boarder analyze the pill I found and he told me it's homemade. He says all the Nazi bigshots knew how to make them for emergencies."

Slowing down, Roth pulled to a stop on the soft shoulder, then turned to face me. "Zack, how many times do I have to tell you? There's a right way to do things and a wrong way."

I could smell another lecture coming on.

". . . we've *got* to stick to proper legal procedures or any evidence we gather will be thrown out of court," he said, then resumed driving. "As it is, that pill of yours is inadmissible evidence."

"What does that mean?"

"It means that it was gathered illegally and won't be recognized as valid proof of anything. That's why I keep telling you. Everything has to be on the up and up."

"I guess I got a carried away. Sorry."

I asked him to park around the corner so that my folks wouldn't spot us. When I returned, Roth remained quiet for a long time. Finally, he cracked a grin.

"Your boarder's probably wondering where the hell you got hold of a cyanide tablet."

I explained my rat-poison story, and was surprised that Roth seemed to approve. As we neared Smith's Pond, he said, "We're still a long way from an arrest, Zack. Just knowing the whereabouts of an alleged Nazi is only half the battle." Roth's by-the-book method was beginning to drive me bananas. "First we've got to find out who he is and what he's doing in Oakville," he said. "Then we've got to be able to *prove* this guy is really a Nazi officer. And right now, it looks like Bondi was the only person who could have done that."

"You still think Big Lew was trying to shut Buddy up?"

"Possibly," he said. "But it could've been an outside deal . . . The one thing we have to keep in mind is that the Bondi murder may not be related to the Nazi angle. I may be totally off. I sure hope not, but then again, you never know."

The relentless cold over the past few weeks had frozen the pond solid except for some spots in the middle where the ice remained only an inch or so thick. Usually after school kids would be playing a pickup game of hockey, but the place was abandoned when Roth and I arrived.

It was a well-known fact that Keller had no qualms about dumping factory poisons into the water; nobody dared go near the place in the summer—the shore looked like a fish graveyard. The townspeople regularly made a big issue of the pond. But each time the complaints were squelched by Keller and Wentworth, and the plant would resume spilling poisons and billowing smoke. At least with the water frozen and the shore hidden by snow, the pond was actually a nice place for kids to play.

It was too cramped to put our skates on in the Packard, so we braved the cold and laced up outside. Roth was having problems with his wounded arm but was too stubborn to ask for help.

"No stick?" I said, as we hit the ice.

"I don't own one."

I was impressed by the lieutenant's coordination and speed, and wondered if I could beat him in a little one-on-one. From where we were skating, I had a clear view of both Oakville Textile and Keller Plastic. As Roth was cutting some figure eights, something caught my eye. Big Lew had just left the Keller offices and was headed towards the Olds coupe parked in the adjoining lot. There was a tall man with him. The coupe looked exactly as it had before the hit-and-run—green and weathered. Gus Olaf had done a good job.

I motioned to Roth, who stopped skating and focused on Heinz in the distance.

"Who's that with him?" Roth asked.

"I don't know, can't tell." I squinted for a better view. "Looks kinda like Mayor Wentworth. "

Roth's eye's narrowed as Heinz and the man drove off and out of sight. With dusk beginning to fall, we decided to call it quits. Heading towards shore, Roth said, "How'd you like to take my daughters skating sometime?"

I told him it was a good idea, but thought to myself that was the last thing I needed.

"C'mon, tough guy," Roth teased, "I'll race you." He took off with a head start. Skating frantically, I finally passed him. But pretty soon he caught up and we both crashed to shore in a blast of snow. Roth laughed and groaned at the same time—he'd fallen on his sore arm. As we removed our skates, though, his mood darkened.

"What's the matter?"

"You're probably going to find this hard to believe, Zack, but whenever I enjoy myself, I can't help but think of my father spending all that time in a concentration camp." He glanced over to check my reaction. Then he grinned, adding, "Must be Jewish guilt."

The drive back was quiet and solemn. Roth was obviously still brooding about his father. Actually, I felt a little guilty, too. There I was having such a good time myself and Buddy was stuck in the hospital.

Thankfully, Roth broke the silence. "I'm curious . . . did they tell you anything in school about the Japanese camps?"

"You mean Japanese concentration camps?"

"The ones in Arizona and Nevada," Roth said. "I'm wondering if they told you the whole story."

"They didn't tell us *any* story."

"Not a word about the camps right here in this country?"

I looked at him, baffled.

"I don't believe it." Roth's eyes were fixed on the road as he continued. "Well, right after Pearl Harbor, America reacted with a gut impulse for revenge," he explained. "So they arrested all the Japanese Americans, confiscated their property and threw them into prison camps for the duration of the war."

I was speechless.

"What about your family?" Roth asked. "Didn't they talk about it?"

"Nope." That was the first time I ever heard about concentration camps in America.

As we continued, silently, I thought about how much I must have been sheltered from the realities of the world. My parents always seemed content to let me live in my radio dreams where the good guys always won and crime didn't pay. I'm sure that keeping the real world a mystery was easier for them.

Roth said a solemn goodbye and dropped me off around the corner from the apartment. Walking home, I began to sense how much I was going to miss Roth when the case was over.

32

On Saturday morning I got the notion to stake out Miss Porter's place. I figured I'd spot Big Lew or Roth, or something interesting anyway. So I lurked in the trees across the street from her house. After about an hour, though, I started to lose my enthusiasm as my feet went numb with cold. Then a voice pierced the air.

"Zack!"

It was Porky Olaf. He was wearing his overstuffed leather cap with the earmuffs, and he had a big yellow scarf wrapped around his neck and half his face. He looked like a big goof, but he was probably as warm as toast while I was out there freezing my ass off.

Porky was pulling a little wagon containing a car battery. "Listen to this. Hickox' heap won't start," he said. "Gotta replace the battery. Ol' one's no fuckin' good."

Porky passed by without another word. And I continued with my watch. After another half hour, I decided to warm up and have lunch. So I went to Lucky Pierre's—a neighborhood diner that always smelled of cabbage—and blew my movie money on soup and a burger, which was gray and spongy. No doubt it was called Lucky Pierre's because you were pretty damn lucky if the food didn't kill you. At least the diner was heated, though, and I was able to thaw out before returning to my stakeout.

Unfortunately, it didn't take long before my hands, nose and feet began to freeze again. Then, just as I was about to leave for home, the Packard pulled up to Miss Porter's house. I stepped back into the shadows.

Roth didn't get right out of the car but instead fussed with something beside him on the seat. Then he adjusted the rearview mirror and proceeded to fix his tie and examine his teeth. Finally, he climbed from the car carrying a small, nicely wrapped package. He paused and looked up and down the street before proceeding to Miss Porter's door and knocking. She answered, all smiles, and they disappeared inside.

My body temperature shot up instantly. Even though I couldn't see what was happening, my imagination filled in the sordid details.

Mary Beth would help Roth off with his coat. She'd be freshly bathed and smelling of lilacs. Then, after a little chitchat she'd excuse herself. Pausing at the record player, she'd flip on Chopin's Polonaise and smile coyly before ducking into the kitchen. Roth would sneak a last look at himself in the mirror over the mantel, check out his hair and loosen his tie.

Miss Porter would emerge from the kitchen wearing a silk negligee and carrying a tray with wine instead of coffee. "I figured you to be a wine man," she'd say breathlessly. "You figured right," Roth would say, then take her in his arms and they'd kiss. The wine glasses would slide to the floor and crash. But they'd just laugh and continue smooching.

After a few moments of torturous silence, I thought I could actually hear the sound of their passionate breathing.

"Zack!" It was Porky again, pulling his wagon back the other way with Hickox's dead battery. "Still won't start," he reported. "Listen to this. My ol' man's gonna have to tow it now. Oh, boy!"

"Probably ready for the junkyard," I grumbled.

"Prob'bly."

As soon as Porky was gone, Roth left the house and re-entered his car. It looked to me like he was wiping lipstick from his mouth.

∽ᚹ

Rocky Graziano was voted "Boxer of the Year" in '45. Along with Willie Pep, the "Rock" was my favorite fighter. A tough street brawler with a colorful style, Graziano fascinated me. Tales that he spent most of his delinquent youth in prison and had lost several of his childhood pals to various kinds of sudden death—including the electric chair—only added to the myth.

Rocky's favorite line was, "I eat welterweights for breakfast." And I used to get a big kick out of his post-fight radio interviews. "What? what? what?" Rocky would say. When asked about his opponent, he'd answer, "Yeah, he was mahvelous, mahvelous. But I killed da bum . . . heh, heh, heh."

I began to wonder if I'd ever get to Madison Square Garden with Roth, or if he had promised that treat just to make sure I'd testify. I also wondered if maybe he had promised treats to Miss Porter, too. As I lay in bed worrying about Roth and Miss Porter again, I realized that my image of the lieutenant was changing. He was no longer the scrappy hero from my radio favorites—Roth had become just another Joe, who happened to be a detective. No longer was he someone to idolize, but simply one to respect. And for the first time I understood that my friendship with the lieutenant *wasn't* the answer to all my problems. Needless to say, I didn't fall asleep until after midnight.

Climbing through the thick ropes I could hear the announcer, who looked a little like Popovich, shout: "Weighing in at eighty-nine pounds, with purple trunks . . . from Oakville, Connecticut . . . *"ZACK THE KNIFE SILVER!"*

There were scattered boos. I'd called myself "Zack, The Knife" in dreams before. Not only had I used that nickname as a prizefighter, but also as a football hero, to describe my slashing moves through defensive lines.

As I danced around the ring warming up, I caught the eye of Miss Porter and Melissa, who were sitting together in the crowd. They were whispering and giggling like silly schoolgirls. "Grow up!" I shouted, but it was lost in the crowd noise. A few rows behind them, Lenny was seated between Birdwell and Porky, looking something like the Ritz Brothers.

My mother was my second, my father was my trainer. Roth, blowing smoke rings, was at ringside nervously puffing a long seegar as if he had a big stake on the fight. His twin daughters, stuffing their cheeks with popcorn, were seated on either side of him and I was convinced they were eyeing me with contempt.

The Popovich look-alike continued to roar: "And weighing in at two hundred and forty-five pounds, in brown trunks . . . from The Oakville Police Department . . . *BIG LEW HEINZ!*"

The crowd's deafening applause woke me, and I found it impossible to fall asleep again.

33

Nearly everyone in Oakville dressed up on Sunday to celebrate the weekend. But I was feeling too miserable to join in, what with my so-called partner hobnobbing with the only woman I truly loved, and my best friend in the hospital with the possibility of never walking again.

"At least he's alive," my father said. "You can be grateful for that."

I agreed that Buddy being alive was good reason for thanks. "But still . . ." Forgoing breakfast at home, I decided to visit Buddy at St. Luke's.

As I hurried down the hospital corridor, the Goodsons were just leaving. Buddy's father deftly avoided my eyes. Following the accident, he'd been acting strangely cool. But I said "Hi," anyway, and sneaked a peek back at Claire as they headed outside. She was blossoming into a real beauty and I knew that meant her football days with the boys, and my free feelies along with them, were probably over.

Buddy was resting when I entered the room. He didn't look well. The breakfast was cold and untouched on his tray. He hardly even smiled when I greeted him. "What's with the long face?" I could also tell he'd been crying.

"Heinz's lawyer came by last night. And he asked an awful lot of questions."

I immediately feared the worst.

"He kept bugging me about the day Popovich gave me those Old Golds."

"Why do you think you're here?" I tried to explain. "Popovich told Big Lew you were around that day, so he probably figures you saw the murder."

"But I told Roth that Heinz wasn't driving the car!"

I eyed Buddy's breakfast. "Did the lawyer say anything about me?" I asked.

"Didn't I tell you?"

I shook my head.

"Well, he knew we were together after school," Buddy said, "but nothing else. Popovich didn't tell Heinz he saw you, just me."

Slightly relieved, I helped myself to the orange juice without asking.

"This lawyer guy just kept saying, 'Is there anything else you want to tell me?' He said that about a hundred times."

I tried to swallow the juice, but couldn't. "What else did you tell him?"

"Just that we were together. I was too scared to lie, Zack. He would've known. He's a lawyer."

"Yeah," I said, "but he's *Heinz's* lawyer."

Buddy didn't seem to understand. I felt sorry for him though, and decided to change the subject. "How 'bout a little exercise?"

A grin appeared on his face. "Long as it ain't one-on-one."

I helped Buddy into his wheelchair and pushed him down the corridor to the physical therapy room. Picking up speed down the passageway, we whipped around the corner and just made it through the doorway. We broke up laughing for the first time in weeks.

I switched on the lights. "I bet we'll be skating together at Smith's Pond before it thaws."

"Well we sure as hell ain't skating there *after* it thaws," he kidded. I grinned, glad he was back to his old self—if not physically, at least mentally.

Then, with a specific plan in mind, I helped position Buddy between the arms of two exercise bars. I could see the doubt on his face, so I cracked the latest gag that was going around. "You know what Hitler's last words to Goering were as the Russian's were closing in?"

"I'll bite."

I did my best German accent. "I've got der blues, Hermann!"

Buddy looked at me deadpan, then he giggled.

"Okay," I said, "now let's see what you've got." I stepped back to the wall to watch. "Try pulling yourself up with your arms. So use the bars to help."

He took a deep breath, grabbed hold of the bars, grimaced, and hauled himself up.

"Not bad . . ."

I could see he was gritting his teeth as he shuffled slowly forward. But there was a new glimmer of hope on his face. "Okay, now let yourself go and come over here."

Buddy was perspiring. Then he forced a grin and started. Taking one step, he teetered, then crumbled to the floor, face down, as though he'd been shot. He was shaking and sobbing, his head buried in both arms. Feeling unsteady myself, I leaned back and slid down the wall, then bit the inside of my cheek trying to hold back the tears.

∽⊁

"The Fred Allen Show" was yet another Silver family ritual. We loved Allen's ongoing rivalry with Jack Benny. My parents especially liked a Jewish character on the show called Mrs. Nussbaum, who'd answer her door with, "You were expecting maybe the Fink Spots?" or, "You were expecting maybe the King Cohen Trio?" Mrs. Nussbaum also referred to "mine husband, Pierre," which always drew chuckles from my folks.

In the wake of the PT Room disaster, I decided to stay late at St. Luke's and listen to the "Fred Allen Show" with Buddy. He wasn't that big on Mrs. Nussbaum, but he loved a character called Senator Claghorn. The Senator, newest member of Allen's wild cast, was already being mimicked by everybody at school. Even the intern, who had dropped in to examine Buddy, did a bad imitation.

Claghorn, who carried Southernhood about as far as it could go, told how he was weaned on mint juleps, drank only from a Dixie cup, saw only Ann Sothern movies, never-ever listened to Mr. & Mrs. North, avoided the Lincoln Tunnel at all costs, and *always* wore a Kentucky derby. That night, the senator really got going:

"Claghorn's the name! Senator Claghorn, that is. Ah'm from Dixie. And Ah represent the South!"

Allen tried to butt in. "Look Senator, I . . ."

Claghorn shot back: "Thanksgivin' Ah only eat the part of the turkey that's facin' south."

"Y-Yes, b-but . . ."

"No man livin' can make me wear a Union suit!"

"W-Well, I . . ."

"What's on your mind, son? Speak up! This is America, son. You got free speech. Go ahead and talk, son!"

The nurse had to come in and stop us from guffawing because the man next door had just come out of surgery. But she agreed to let us listen to the rest of the show after Buddy promised we'd keep it "real quiet." It was obvious the nurse had a soft spot for Buddy.

I had a soft spot for Buddy, too. And as I left the hospital to head home, I prayed for the time when he would be better and we'd be back playing basketball and hockey. My initial anger over Buddy spilling his guts to Big Lew's lawyer had long since passed. After all, Buddy hadn't even *seen* the killing, so for him to get smashed up like he did was totally unjust. If anyone should have got run down, it was me. But I'll never forget something Roth told me after the accident: "Never question fate—you won't get a straight answer."

34

I awoke in the middle of the night to the sounds of commotion. At first I wasn't sure if it was my imagination—the noises were both real and terrible. But it was shadowy dark, and the hall light seeping under the door into my room cast a strange glow at the foot of the bed. It seemed like another nightmare.

I could distinctly hear someone groaning and crying out in pain. Throwing off my covers, I went for the door. As I stood in the hallway, my mother rushed past me, hysterical. I saw my father's feet protruding from the bathroom doorframe and I immediately knew that something awful was happening. My mother kneeled awkwardly beside him, weeping uncontrollably. I knew right then and there that this was no nightmare.

My first impulse was to return to bed. I wasn't exactly sure what was happening, and I didn't want to know. I just wanted to bury myself under the covers and wait for the sun to bring a new day. But hearing Lenny made me stay. He sounded panicked as he sputtered our address over the phone. His words were barely audible over my father's groans, but I could hear that his voice, usually so cool, had been replaced by a soft stammering. It took him three tries to get our address right, then he hung up and rushed into the bathroom.

I stepped a little closer, still confused. I wanted to shout out for my father to stop groaning, but nothing came out of my mouth. I wanted to cry, but it was as if I had forgotten how. That's when Lenny spotted me and eased me back to my room.

"Go back to bed, Zack."

"Is he gonna be okay?"

"Just go back to bed." Lenny closed the door softly, and I could hear him comforting my mother in the hallway. I could hear the sobs and whispers. Standing in the dark, cold bedroom, I pictured my father lying on the cold tile bathroom floor, gulping air. Collapsing onto my bed, I felt short of breath and forced myself to breath slowly and deeply. That's the last thing I remember until Lenny awoke me hours later.

❦

The sun was just beginning to rise, as Lenny, silhouetted against the dull orange sky outside, sat on the edge of my bed. The events of the night before were muddled and I was uncertain how much I had dreamed and how much had really happened. Lenny looked uneasy, his head lowered.

"Is Dad okay?"

Tugging on his hair as though he was trying to hide his face behind it, he explained that our father had suffered a massive heart attack. Then he added, "Mom called and wants us at the hospital soon as possible."

I felt a sudden chill, and started shaking. "What should I wear?"

"I don't know, Zack. It really doesn't matter." He rose from the bed and wandered out of the room.

I wrapped myself in my blanket and moved over to the closet. But there was nothing I could find to wear. As I searched through my things, I felt tears rolling down my cheeks. And pretty soon I was bawling. I couldn't find anything appropriate to put on. I wanted something that would make my father proud, but I couldn't come up with anything. So I just stood there, crying, until Lenny returned and silently helped me into a warm sweater and pants.

We set off walking to the hospital in the early light of dawn. Keeping up with Lenny was difficult for me. It was bitter cold and the steam of our breath quickly evaporated as we hustled through the quiet streets to the hospital. The image of my father gasping for air became even more real, and I started crying again. The tears trickling down my face warmed my frozen cheeks. When Lenny noticed, he slowed down and placed a comforting arm on my shoulder. I think that was the first time I really felt love from him.

We arrived at the hospital just as the sun was fully up, glowing and beautiful. My mother was waiting outside the hospital in the parking lot and we moved silently to her side. Her eyes were moist and swollen. She wasn't crying. She had no tears left. "Your father's dead," she said, opening her arms wide and embracing us.

∞

For me, the Jewish custom of burying the dead as quickly as possible was both confusing and frustrating. The last thing I wanted was for my father to disappear so fast.

Memorial services were held the very next day at Temple Beth Zion in Waterbury. Rabbi Schecter, Glick's superior, presided. I took some pleasure seeing Glick in a subservient position, and was even surprised at how nice he was to me for a change. In addition to our immediate family, Roth attended, along with countless others from town. I never realized my father was so well liked.

The lieutenant was seated behind me, patting me on the arm occasionally. Buddy came, too. It was his first outing since the accident. He looked uncomfortable cramped in his wheelchair and wearing a yarmulke, but he kept telling his mother he wanted to stay until the end.

"Bert was a wonderful guy," the mourners said. "Don't ever forget that, Zachary." Or, "I knew your father for years. He was a wonderful man." Almost everyone added, "Don't ever forget that."

I promised I wouldn't.

I saw uncles and aunts I'd never met before, relatives who drove in from Bridgeport, Brooklyn, and from as far off as Philadelphia. Even my father's older brother, Norman, attended, though he hadn't spoken with the family in years.

The burial took place later that same day at a large cemetery on Long Island. The drive there seemed endless as we trekked through a heavy snowfall. The limousine carrying the immediate family trailed the hearse, preceding a long line of cars. Riding with my uncle Norman, who was loud and had terrible breath, made a miserable situation that much worse.

"Why not bury him in Oakville?" he had to ask.

"Because Bert wanted to be in the family plot on Long Island," my mother snapped.

"I don't see what's wrong with Oakville," he mumbled.

No one said much after that, and I could finally see why my mother never spoke to Uncle Norman. I could also see that she was devastated. Since Lenny was off in his own world, staring out the window with his nose against the glass, I moved closer to my mother and placed a hand on her lap.

By the time we arrived at the grave site it was already dark and the falling snow had turned to sleet. But they proceeded with the ceremony anyway. I remember it had all happened too fast. I had wanted so much to tell my father all the things I never told him. I wanted to say goodbye and I wanted him to look back and let me know that everything was going to be all right.

35

Roth had pulled Lenny aside at the funeral and offered to extend his help. "I really feel sorry for the kid," he said, "he deserves a helluva lot better." Knowing that I would've liked to hear that, Lenny graciously passed it on. Still, no amount of sympathy was going to make the situation any easier to swallow.

After a week had passed, along with a lot of tears, the time came to return to school. I knew I had to put the past behind me and move forward. On my way to Baldwin that first day, though, I wondered about the future. I was worried that Roth would not be able to gather enough hard evidence before the trial if he continued insisting that everything be done "by the book." The way I saw it, Big Lew and some vicious Nazi were still out there, ready to kill me. I didn't give a fig about his "book." And I determined that if Roth couldn't wrap up the case pretty soon, I wasn't going to hesitate in coming up with my own plan. The frustration and anger were building inside me. I wanted someone to pay for my father's death and my best friend's accident. I wanted to nail Big Lew and work things out with Miss Porter—in that order.

My mother tried to remain enthusiastic about my upcoming bar mitzvah. But that was the last thing on my mind. During the time I'd been absent from school, I started an enormous painting about my life in Oakville. It was the one way I could vent my feelings concerning my father and the case.

Although I intended the painting to be in the style of Norman Rockwell, it ended up looking more like something by Grandma Moses. All the events and activities were depicted in a kind of primitive, comic strip format. I illustrated both the good times and the bad times: home and school, my friendship with Buddy, swimming at Black Rock and our heated contests in basketball and hockey. I even painted the scene of Bondi and Miss Porter under the old oak behind the gym, as well as Bondi's murder, with Ryan handcuffed to a nearby tree. In the bottom right corner, I rendered my impression of Buddy getting clipped by the Olds. In the bottom left, I depicted my father's death. When I finished, I covered several sections of the picture with black triangles and rectangles. These were scenes I didn't want anybody to see.

Although the picture looked odd—peppered with black shapes—I was proud of the effort and couldn't resist telling Miss Porter about it.

"I'd love to see it, Zachary. Why don't you bring it over to my place later."

I quickly agreed, and my imagination was off and running. I was already figuring out what I'd say if she asked me to move in with her. But for the remainder of the class, she hardly looked at me. Then it occurred to me that maybe she had asked to see my picture out of pity. At first the thought bothered me, but later I realized "you've got to take it when it comes"—a philosophy Coach Ryan had shared with me in regard to my jump shot. So I raced home after school, brushed my teeth with Pepsodent for that "cleaner, brighter taste," combed my hair, wrapped my painting and headed for the house where Mary Beth lived.

On the way over I ran into Birdwell, carrying skates and a hockey stick. "How come you never skate anymore, Silver?"

"I got better things to do."

"Big deal."

Arriving at Miss Porter's front door, my dream quickly fizzled. She didn't greet me in a negligee. In fact, she wasn't even wearing pumps. She wore scuffed saddle shoes and her body was hidden by an oversized sweater which hung halfway down her legs. I'd hoped for something sexier, but I was excited anyway. As I set my painting down, she asked if I wanted a cup of hot cocoa. I told her I'd love some and followed her into the kitchen. There was a book open at the table, and she caught me peeking at the title.

"*Forever Amber*," she said. "It's a romantic best seller." I sat down and watched her as she prepared the cocoa.

"Love stories are one of my weaknesses," she confessed.

I felt like saying mine was whiskey and women. But I opted for: "Mine's chocolate."

She expressed her sympathy again about my father and reiterated how sorry she felt for me. I thanked her again and told her I'd rather not discuss it. We finally got around to the cocoa and my painting, which she studied for a good five minutes.

"It's marvelous," she finally said. "But what are those black patches?"

"I had to cover some of the things. It's private."

She sat down next to me on the sofa and gazed into my eyes. "I understand," she murmured. Then she rose from her seat, went to the phonograph player and put on a record. It was Sinatra singing "I'll Buy That Dream." She lowered the volume and returned to my side. "I'm glad you express yourself so honestly, Zack."

"Then what about you and Roth?" I blurted, unable to restrain myself.

"What about me and Lieutenant Roth?"

"I know you've been seeing each other."

Her mouth dropped open.

"I don't trust him," I said. "Not around you, anyway. I'll bet you didn't even know he's married."

She cracked a slight grin. "My goodness, you're jealous."

"You bet I am."

"Well, you're wrong about Lieutenant Roth. He's just doing his job. Yes, he has been here a lot, but only to ask questions about Officer Heinz." She looked at me seriously. "He happens to trust you very much, Zachary."

"Yeah, because he needs me."

"Not just that. I thinks he feels you're very special. Like the son he's always wanted."

I honestly had never thought about it that way before. But I sort of enjoyed the idea of Roth as my ol' man—not a father exactly, but more like someone in between a father and Lenny, a kind of big brother you respect.

Since we were baring so much soul, I had no qualms about my next question. "How 'bout you and Big Lew? He just doing his job, too?"

Her face went rosy, and I feared that I'd pushed too far. After an awkward pause, she stood up and moved to the fireplace mantel. I figured she didn't want to talk about Heinz; then she turned back and looked into my eyes. "No, he's not doing his job, unless his job is blackmailing me."

I tried to contain my surprise by forcing a cough.

"Somebody should know the truth, and it might as well be you, Zachary. I can trust you can't I?"

I nodded vigorously.

Then she gazed over at an old family photo hanging near the fireplace as she revealed the details: "Five years ago, when I was seventeen, my brother, Dwayne, somehow persuaded me to drive his get-away car in an armed robbery. He was always a problem kid, but I think he just wanted so much to make something of himself. Anyway, we stopped at that Texaco station outside of town on Route 8. You know the one?"

I was absolutely thrilled by the idea of my art teacher behind the wheel of a roadster in an armed garage heist. "I always thought you were a terrific driver."

She forced a smile. "I guess Dwayne did, too." There was a brief silence, then she resumed. "Unfortunately, my brother didn't tell me about the armed robbery part. I thought he was just buying a pack of cigarettes. So when he jumped back into the car with a bag of money in one hand and a pistol in the other, I nearly fainted. I couldn't think straight. All I remember was flooring the gas pedal and speeding off."

I had never seen Miss Porter look so vulnerable and exciting as she did then. She reminded me of Lana Turner or Joan Crawford in some gangster movie.

"Needless to say, Heinz caught us right after I crashed the car." Then she sighed. "It was very embarrassing. There was a quick trial and Dwayne went to prison."

"What happened to you?" I asked, studying her mouth.

"I was just about to enter teacher's college in New Britain. Everything was all set and my future looked great. Heinz said he'd give me a chance, and I remember the words to this day. He said, 'I'll be keeping an eye on you, every part of you.' " She paused to sigh. "And I knew exactly what he meant."

"That letch!"

"For four years, I never heard from him. Then, when this teaching job brought me back to Oakville," she said, "he blackmailed me into seeing him, saying that he'd make sure my brother never got out. And if I didn't cooperate, he'd reopen the case and send me to prison too."

I was extremely curious just how much she had to "cooperate," but I refrained from asking. Instead, I said: "Where's Dwayne now?"

"He's still serving time in Danbury. He'll be eligible for parole next Spring."

Then she volunteered: "I think Heinz must hate me now as much as I hate him. He's such a jealous man, Zack. And as hard as it is to admit it, I know I've done things just to hurt him.'' I began to feel like a heel for thinking she'd ever fool around with Roth—or willingly with Big Lew for that matter. But I figured she was feeling pretty guilty herself.

Finally, she returned to the sofa, sat down and put her hands on my shoulders before I could move. I could smell the lilac perfume and see the moisture on her lips. ''You're the only one who knows my secret, Zachary. Not even Lieutenant Roth knows.'' Her breath was sweet and inviting. ''And I wish you were ten years older so I could share something else with you . . .''

''T-Ten years is a long time.''

Slowly, softly, she leaned close and planted her mouth on mine. It seemed like someone had turned up the volume on the phono—but it must have been my imagination. The kiss, though, was real.

36

Sitting in class the next day I decided that all the wrongs in my life had been righted and that Miss Porter was the reward for all my suffering. After our kiss, I assumed everything would be different between us. I envisioned a huge wedding, attended by my family and all our friends, and a five-piece band that would play our song: "I'll Buy That Dream." After our honeymoon, I could just see it: she would write "Mary Beth Silver" on the chalkboard, making sure that all the students got it right.

But something was screwy. My bride-to-be smiled at me pleasantly, but nothing more. No sloe-eyed grin. No special attention. Had she forgotten our kiss? Had she spoken to Roth, or made up with Big Lew? My head was spinning. Needless to say, I learned little at school that day. At least, after the final bell, I was relieved not to find Roth waiting at his usual spot outside.

Later, when I returned from Hebrew school, I decided to take in a little skating at Smith's Pond before dinner. Hardly anyone was around, except a few high school kids playing hockey, which was lucky because I had some serious thinking to do. As the sun began to set, the players disappeared. Ever since I was old enough to skate I had dreamed of having the ice to myself. But now that I had it, it was lonely and scary. What if I fell in? I thought. Who was going to pull me out?

Although the ice looked fairly smooth, I kept a sharp eye out for rocks and debris, haunted by all the skating accidents that had occurred there. Within minutes my fingers started to numb from the cold, so I skated ashore to build a little fire, something Buddy and I had often done. Sometimes we'd bring potatoes, toss them into the embers, then gobble them up. I was only interested in warming up, though. So I removed my gloves and began rubbing my hands over the heat.

My father and I had done the same thing after ice fishing at Black Rock when I was nine. I still remember the deal we made: "I'll hook your worm if you light the fire." I hated worms, couldn't touch them. On the other hand, my father had this fear about matches, something that went back to when he was a boy and nearly burned his family's house down.

As I sat there warming up, a gunshot sounded across the lake and whizzed past my ear, blasting a chunk of bark from the tree behind me. I didn't move a muscle, but my heart was thumping wildly. Suddenly, another shot ripped into the snow and earth at my feet. Panicking, I dove into a nearby gully, closed my eyes and prayed—not to God, but to my father. I was certain he was watching over me. Finally, I heard a car rev and roar away somewhere across the pond.

Getting up on shaky legs, I made my way to the shattered tree. Lodged in the trunk was a spent round. Using my Ranger Knife, I removed the slug and pocketed it. As I hustled home, I kept an eye out for the Olds or Big Lew. World War II was over all right, but Oakville had become a battle zone.

For the time being, my mother hired Brad Bailey, a young man with curly hair and a silly moustache, to work in the store until she could figure out what to do for the long haul. She had already admitted she was considering selling Silver's General, which no doubt would mean moving out of Oakville. She even spoke of resettling in Brooklyn or Long Island, to be closer to her sisters. None of those possibilities excited me tremendously. And as far as Bailey was concerned, I disliked him from the start. I hated his phony smile, good cheer and flirty way with my mother; he had trouble looking anyone in the eye when he spoke—except her. I also resented the fact that my mother didn't seem to be mourning much since the funeral.

Before I went upstairs, Bailey informed me that Lenny was still at band rehearsal and that my mother had a late business appointment in Waterbury with the lawyer. There was no sign of Maibaum.

"How 'bout a game of checkers?" Bailey asked. "I hear you're not bad."

"No thanks." The idea of competing with him riled me.

As soon as I got to the phone upstairs, I dialed Roth's home number. While it was ringing, I mulled over how I was going to dramatize the attempt on my life.

"Hello?" It was Roth's wife.

I asked if I could speak with the lieutenant.

"Harry's not home." Her voice sounded sweet, and I wondered what she looked like.

"This is Zack Silver."

"Zachary! Harry's told me about you."

"Really?" I could hear the twins in the background. "Do you have a number where to reach him? It's an emergency. About the case . . ."

Before hanging up, she said she was looking forward to meeting me. I told her thanks, then dialed Roth's number.

After one ring, a deep-voiced man answered. "Federal Bureau of Investigation."

I was speechless.

Upon giving the man my name, I was transferred to an agent, who listened to my story patiently. Finally, he said, "I understand, son. We know exactly what's going on."

"Can't I speak with Lieutenant Roth?"

"I'm afraid he's on special assignment in Washington right now. But I can assure you he'll be in touch within the next forty-eight hours. My advice is to stay at home out of sight."

"Thank you," I said, a bag of nerves.

"Anything else?"

There was a lot I wanted to say, but I wanted to say it to Roth.

37

When Oklahoma A & M beat Mikan and the DePaul Blue Demons in the NIT playoffs, I barely took notice—sports had been relegated to a lesser priority. Despite my heavy schedule, I still intended to play varsity ball the following year. By then, I figured Corky Pope would be history and Coach Ryan would be back at the helm. I hadn't seen Ryan since visiting him shortly after the murder, but I could just imagine how dejected he felt being cooped up through the holidays. So I decided it was time to drop in on him again.

As I approached the old jailhouse, I wondered if all the publicity might actually help Ryan's election chances when he got out. He thanked me for the bag of peanuts I'd brought him and we chatted about sports for awhile. Munching away, Ryan asked if it was true that five players from Brooklyn College had been expelled in a big scandal, for taking bribes. Regretfully, I told him that it was.

"I tell you, kid," Ryan said, "the whole world's going to hell." Then, he started ranting about "Oakville's great decline," all the while polishing off the peanuts. "I'm worried, kid. Heinz and the mayor are a two-headed monster that's gonna eat this town alive."

I had actually met Mayor Wentworth when he visited Baldwin to hand out some sports awards, and he had seemed like a nice enough man. But Ryan saw the wolf beneath the sheep's clothing.

"Wentworth's arranged for this hotshot lawyer from Bridgeport to represent Heinz," Ryan grumbled.

"Buddy already met him," I said. "And he says the guy's got a real way of getting you to say things you don't mean."

Ryan paused and straightened as if he were addressing voters. "If I ever get to be mayor, I'm gonna clean up this town once and for all."

I didn't doubt that for one minute.

As I headed home later, the Packard passed me, going in the opposite direction. The brakes screeched and Roth hung his head out the window. "Want a lift?" In my wildest dreams I never imagined I'd get to cruise around Oakville in a slick car with a federal agent.

"I had a little business out of town," Roth said as we drove towards Main Street. "But I'm glad to see you're okay." Then he told me that he'd heard about the attempt on my life.

"Yeah," I said. "And if the guy was a decent shot, I wouldn't be here now." I held out the bullet I'd dug from the tree. Roth examined it in between glances at the road.

"It was probably just meant to scare you."

"Well, it sure as hell worked."

"I'll bet we can run a make on this at headquarters," Roth said, eyeing the bullet. "It's definitely not American. Looks like it might've come from a Mauser." Pocketing it, he grinned. "I suppose by now you know I'm with the Bureau."

"Yeah," I said, with as much fake indifference as I could manage.

"I've been getting a lot of heat from the top to bring in my man before the upcoming war crime trials in Germany," he explained. "I know I've put you in a difficult position, Zack. But without you, God knows how long this would've taken."

It felt good to be appreciated.

"I've decided," he said. "We're moving in to grab the Nazi tonight at nine."

"At last," I said, trying to mask my excitement.

"We ran a check on 135 Maple and discovered that the property is owned by Heinz," Roth said. "But when we examined his bank account, there was no rent being paid in for that address. Then we turned up some cashed Keller Plastic checks. And on the back of the checks, one employee gave his current address as 135 Maple."

I listened intently as he unraveled the mystery.

"His name is Carl Frederick," Roth continued.

"Sounds German to me."

Roth nodded.

"I don't know if I can get out after dinner tonight," I said. "But I'll sure as heck try."

Roth gave me a quizzical look. "Who said anything about *you*?" I looked away. "You can't go, Zack," he said flatly.

"What about Big Lew?"

"We'll pick him up right after we get the Nazi. If Heinz doesn't collect rent, we can bring him in for harboring an enemy. Once he's behind bars, we'll formally charge him with the murder. That way, you're safe."

I vainly tried to conceal my disappointment. "And what am I supposed to do, hide under my bed while you're having all the fun?"

As we pulled to a stop around the corner from the store he sighed. "I'm only trying to protect you, Zack."

"Then why didn't you tell me you work for the F.B.I.?"

Taking a deep breath, he faced me squarely. "I know how difficult things have been, Zack. But I had to make sure I could trust you before you found out. If word leaked that there was a federal agent in Oakville, Frederick might've taken off." Roth reached out and fidgeted with the Star of David dangling from the rearview. "Look, this is very important to me," he said. "And everything has to go like clockwork. Everything's got to be perfect. There's just no need for another man tonight. Besides, if there's the slightest chance you might get hurt, I don't want you there. I'm sure Frederick's not going to come in without a fight, not to mention Heinz." Then Roth placed a hand on my shoulder. "Your part in all this is finished now, Zachary."

"What if I don't want my part to be over?"

He gazed at me somewhat impatiently. "Look, I just don't need your help tonight. Okay?"

"So, you're f-firing me?" I could feel myself tearing. I couldn't believe it. I'd given up so much for Roth and his precious case: basketball, girls, all that time spying and staking out, not to mention my own safety. "Don't you even need me as a witness anymore?" I had resorted to whining.

"Of course. I just don't want to jeopardize your safety before the trial."

That's when I started crying, my nose running freely. For the first time with Roth I felt like a little kid. I was embarrassed, angry and flustered all at once. "S-So, I'm too young to help with all the good stuff, b-but old enough to tell some crummy jury what I saw. Right?"

Roth watched me sniveling and shaking as I climbed out of the car. "Sorry it had to end like this, Zack."

Trying to control my fury, I stomped towards the apartment, fists clenched.

"I'll probably be too busy to phone tonight," Roth called out. "But I'll catch you first thing in the morning and tell you everything."

I whirled around. "Forget it! I'll read about it in the paper like everybody else!"

He closed the car door and pulled away.

I knew that if I'd returned home with watery eyes, my mother would have bombarded me with questions. So I waited for the tears to stop, then rubbed snow over my face to look like I'd been hit by a vicious gust.

The Christmas decorations my father had put up a couple of days after Thanksgiving were blinking colorfully in the store window. Christmas in Oakville had always been my favorite time of year. Ever since I was little, we'd celebrated the holiday season. My father had tried to teach me about Chanukah, but it never had any real meaning, probably because there were no other Jewish kids around to share it with.

Bailey, grinning as usual, greeted me from behind the counter. "Your mom told me you could have whatever your little heart desires tonight."

I knew damn well she wouldn't have said that, and the idea of Bailey appealing to my "little heart," irked me. "How 'bout a nice chocolate soda, Zack?"

"No thanks," I said. "You know where my mother is?"

"I believe she's got another business meeting in Waterbury. Said she won't be home till late." Bailey's syrupy manner almost made me sick.

Walking slowly upstairs, I considered the desperate state of my life: No father. Buddy out of action. Mother always busy. Brother not concerned. Roth firing me. Miss Porter out of reach. And Big Lew trying to kill me. I don't know why exactly, but I determined that a stiff drink was the answer. I'd never tried the hard stuff, only a sip of wine on special occasions. But at that moment I was more than ready for a "good belt," as my father used to say. So I popped the apartment light on and headed for the top cupboard. Inside the cabinet door a half-filled quart of Ron Rico rum stared me down, beckoning. I was hoping for a whole bottle, but I settled for what was there.

38

By 8:30, I'd finished off most of the rum, and feeling inordinately mellow, tuned in for some radio. Fortunately, there was no sign of Lenny or my mother, although I did hallucinate my brother's smirking face in the rum bottle. "When Irish Eyes are Smiling" dipped under and gave way to "Duffy's Tavern," where you heard the sound of a phone ringing and a receiver being picked up by Archie. "Hello, Duffy's Tavern, where the elite meet to eat. Archie the manager speaking. Duffy ain't here. Oh, hello Duffy . . ." Archie usually made me chuckle, but with everything beginning to whirl around the room I was just too dizzy to enjoy the program.

At 8:45, I stumbled to my room. Though my brain felt stuck in low gear, I had a definite plan to carry out. Pulling an old trunk from under my bed, I flipped it open and started rummaging. I used the trunk to store odd bits of clothing and things for Halloween and other costume occasions.

I hastily slipped one of my mother's discarded dresses over my head then plunked on one of her old, wide-brimmed hats. Determined to follow through with my scheme, I grabbed my pedometer and compass, pocketed them, turned off the radio, then headed for Maple Street.

The rum had left me woozy. But in a way, I felt relaxed. Luckily, it was unseasonably warm outside. Otherwise I would have frozen in my skimpy disguise. On the way, almost everyone I passed did a double take, but no one seemed to recognize me. I tried to keep my stride steady and even—at its usual 25 inches—because my pedometer worked best that way. Understandably, I was having trouble walking a straight line. With each step, I could hear the gadget ticking while recording the distance from our apartment to the house on Maple Street.

It was 8:55 when I arrived at my designated hiding spot—where I'd seen Heinz's mother enter the house that first time. At 8:58, Roth's car pulled to a silent stop across the street. Another sedan pulled in quietly behind "The Pack."

Four men, including Roth, quickly emerged from the vehicles and huddled in the shadows. They spoke in whispers and hand gestures. Finally, Roth pointed in the direction of the mystery house.

Though it was dark, I could just make out that two of the men were carrying rifles. Assuming Roth had his .38 clutched in that gimpy right hand of his, I said a prayer for him to shoot straight. As my excitement grew, I thought of Buddy, and how he would have enjoyed seeing the F.B.I. make their big Nazi arrest. So I made sure to soak up every detail in order that I could retell the story as dramatically as possible.

No one was on the street and there was no traffic. At precisely nine, Roth darted from the car and signaled his men to move in. I watched as the lieutenant kicked open the front door, and followed by the others, stormed inside, yelling.

There was a lot of commotion. One shot was fired. Then there was silence. Suddenly, the light from the house behind me flashed on and I scrambled to another hiding place. A fat man in a robe came out shouting: "What the hell's goin' on!" More silence. Then the man turned and went back inside, muttering curses.

All I could think was, "Who'd been shot?"

Five full minutes elapsed before the answer was made clear. Roth and his men, visibly dejected, finally appeared—just the four of them, with *no prisoner*. Not only was I embarrassed for Roth and the failed raid, but I suddenly felt ridiculous in my mother's dress and hat—not to mention I was feeling blotto.

Making my way back to the apartment, I struggled up the stairs, hoping no one would be home. Sickness swelled in my body, and I vowed to stay away from alcohol forever. As I unlocked the front door and pushed it open, Maibaum's sober mug was there to greet me. Apparently, Lenny was already asleep.

"Hiya, Zack," he said, without so much as a blink. "Your mother called, said she'd be late."

I stood there unsteadily, holding the doorknob for support. But Maibaum didn't notice anything different about me. So I smiled and slurred out, "Good night, David." Retreating to my room, I stashed my pedometer and compass, noting it was exactly one and a half miles to and from the house, S/SE on Maple. I stripped off my costume and slipped into my pajamas. Then, thinking a nice glass of milk could soothe my churning stomach, I staggered into the kitchen. Maibaum, nursing a cup of creamy coffee, was planted at the kitchen table with the newspaper, studying the classified section.

"That new guy's name is Frederick," he said. "Carl

Frederick. I was introduced to him today and, you know, he's not as bad as I made him out to be." Maibaum seemed a little disappointed. "He's just reserved. I mean the guy hardly speaks English. But I'll tell you this much—he really knows his stuff."

"He's German, isn't he?"

"Don't know, haven't heard him really talk."

Pretending I wasn't interested in the subject any longer, I opened the refrigerator. "This all that's left of the milk?"

"Lenny had most of it before he turned in," Maibaum said. "By the way, I'm buying my own from now on so there'll be no more squabbles." He grinned. "It was your mother's idea."

I emptied the milk bottle of what little there was left and spread some peanut butter on a slice of bread. "So you're not mad about this new guy maybe taking your job?"

Maibaum perused an ad that seemed to interest him. "I was mad in the beginning, yes, because it appeared that Keller was pushed into hiring him by Officer Heinz," he said, circling the ad with his pen. "But this Frederick guy knows more than I'll ever know. So how can I complain?"

That Maibaum was such a good sport about being unemployed was surprising. I was curious to know why he thought Heinz had pressured Keller into hiring this Frederick character, but it was time to return to my room. The milk had helped calm my belly, but the peanut butter hadn't.

Crawling under the covers, I scrunched to the middle of my bed and clutched the mattress. The room seemed like it was revolving and I didn't want to go flying off into space. While slipping off to sleep, I began to wonder if Frederick had outsmarted the F.B.I. Maibaum had said he was bright. I imagined him maybe running off to South America, or hiding somewhere in Oakville right under our noses. Nazi or not, Frederick was the least of my problems. Heinz was the real enemy. And I knew he was out there— no doubt waiting to close the book on me.

39

Every year Baldwin Grammar threw a big Christmas Eve party at the school gym which everyone from town attended. And I was especially looking forward to the bash that year. I was planning to ask Roth to attend, as we were encouraged to bring parents; my mother was under the weather with her annual holiday flu.

Following the failed arrest, Roth seemed steadfast, though humbler, and even started treating me with renewed respect. I was hoping my invitation to the party would seal the peace, but he politely declined the offer, saying he was too busy hunting down Frederick, who had apparently vanished into thin air.

"I'm going back to Olaf's Junk today with a few men to really comb the place."

"Watch out for the pooch," I warned, bringing a slight grin to Roth's face.

The dance was a joyous occasion, what with the war over and most of the G.I.'s home. Everybody had something to celebrate. Miss Porter, in a white bare-shouldered gown, looked stunning as she led the glee club in the singing of Christmas music. Down in the audience, Melissa's eyes were fixed lovingly on Buddy in his wheelchair. I was glad for them, but not ready to admit that to anyone but myself.

A gigantic Canadian fir, donated by Oakville Lumber, had been set up on the Visitors' freethrow line. A horde of kids had come by earlier—some with their families—to deck the tree with homemade ornaments and fringe. Even a collection of V-mail, including picture postcards sent from overseas during the war had been placed on the branches. After a few Christmas songs, the high school dance band, with Lenny on sax, began playing fox trots.

Guided by Melissa, Buddy steered his wheelchair straight to the punch and cookies. For a moment, I considered offering Melissa a spin around the dance floor for old time's sake. Instead, I mustered my courage and asked Miss Porter if she'd like to dance.

"Why, I'd love to," she said, taking my sweaty hand.

The band played "Sentimental Journey." With each rotation, I could see Lenny, noticeably shocked, studying us from the bandstand.

"I like the way you lead," Miss Porter whispered.

I spotted Birdwell gossiping with Evette as they peeked over at us. So I pulled Miss Porter closer and danced on dreamily. For the first time in weeks I felt happy and secure.

Suddenly, she stopped dancing. "How 'bout some punch?"

Reluctantly, I agreed, and we made our way to the refreshment table. Grabbing a handful of cookies and two cupfuls of pink juice, I led Miss Porter to a dimly lit area where we could be alone. "Actually, I'd rather be drinking eggnog with hard stuff," I remarked.

She didn't react until after an awkward minute. "I thought you'd like to know I've decided never to see Heinz again."

I was overjoyed.

"He's a cruel man," she continued. "And what's worse, he enjoys it. He's beaten me, you know. Several times."

Then it dawned on me: "That's why you were in the hospital right after the murder, isn't it?"

She lowered her eyes and nodded. "Heinz can't stand the thought of me with any other man," she said, blushing. "In some ways I think my affair with Mr. Bondi was just to make Heinz crazy. But everything backfired."

"What about Roth?" I asked boldly.

She looked at me, then grinned. "I'm very fond of the lieutenant. But there's nothing between us."

I tried to catch her eyes when she said that, but her gaze was lost on something across the gymnasium. And though I *wanted* to believe her, I couldn't. Studying her lovely face, I reached into my sports jacket and removed a small package. "This is for you. Merry Christmas."

She unwrapped it carefully and opened the little box. "Why, it's beautiful!"

I'd bought her a pearl necklace with all my savings, including the money my father had given me toward the purchase of a War Bond. I had ordered it through the mail from the Sunday supplement of the *Courier*, which advertised: "Genuine Imitation Pearl Necklace for the Girl of Your Dreams. Only $9.98!"

"Thank you, Zachary."

I was hoping for a kiss—at least on the cheek. But she only smiled sweetly, saying, "And I've got something for you." Leading me to where she'd left her things, she retrieved a package and presented it to me. I blushed, and tore it open. It was an art book entitled *Cezanne.* My heart sank.

"Cezanne," I said, not sure if that was the right pronunciation. "Wow . . ." I leafed through the pages trying to look interested. In my dreams she had given me some manly aftershave or a personal, sultry photograph with an inscription expressing her deep love for me—but never an art book.

"You wanna dance again?"

"No thanks, Zack, not now." Evidently, she had spotted someone and proceeded to excuse herself. Hurt and embarrassed, I felt like climbing deep inside the branches of the Christmas tree and never coming out.

"Zack!"

I turned to find Buddy beaming up at me from his wheelchair. Melissa was standing behind, but neither of them spoke.

"What's up?" I asked.

"I am," Buddy said. Bracing himself, he rose unsteadily. His eyes were glued to mine and he was shaking with determination. As he stood by himself, Melissa quickly positioned the wheelchair in front of him. Then, lifting his foot, he sent the chair rolling. For a moment, Buddy had to grab onto Melissa for support. But he straightened himself proudly, took three small steps forward, stopped, and turned around. "I've been practicing," he said, "with Melissa's help, of course."

The first thing that came to my mind was that my prayer had worked—that God had really heard me after all. Recalling my vow, I realized that I now owed Buddy a sure win in one-on-one. Just as I was about to congratulate him on the accomplishment, the prettiest girl I'd ever seen appeared next to Melissa and whispered in her ear. They tittered, then Melissa announced: "This is Penny Carrington, from England. She's just moved to America."

Buddy gave me his don't-stand-there-like-a-jerk look, but I was speechless.

"Why don't you ask Penny to dance?" Buddy said.

All I could do was nod, then gesture awkwardly.

"I'd love to," Penny said.

We danced two ballads under Lenny's watchful eye and barely a word was uttered between us—except my occasional, "Sorry, did I step on your toes?"

Later, as we were sipping punch, I spotted Miss Porter standing with some man in the darkness near the fire exit. They were talking intimately. And I watched them giggle as the man slipped his arms over her shoulders. Then I stared dumbfounded as they kissed.

"Would you like to dance another?" Penny asked.

I could only nod distractedly. For a brief moment, I thought the man was Lieutenant Roth; in the darkness it was hard to tell. Actually, the man looked more like Mr. Murphy, Bondi's substitute.

Seeing Miss Porter with Murphy like that didn't rattle me as much as I expected. In a way, I felt a sense of relief. All along I knew, in the back of my mind, that Miss Porter was a dream I might have to one day abandon. Of course, the shock of seeing my bubble burst was somewhat tempered by the arrival of Penny, who was still waiting for our dance. I took a last glance back at the darkened doorway, and saw that Miss Porter and Murphy had disappeared. So I took Penny by the hand and led her onto the dance floor.

∽✿

The day after Christmas Roth stopped by our apartment. My mother answered the door. Still respectful of him—after all, he was a "landsman"—she welcomed the lieutenant's unannounced visit. She showed him into the living room then returned to the kitchen, leaving that door ajar.

I was lying on the carpet sorting my baseball cards, having recently made a big trade with Birdwell in which I got a Dolf Camilli, Pee Wee Reese and Cookie Lavagetto for one rare Van Lingle Mungo in his rookie season with the Giants. Spotting Roth, I quickly stuffed the cards back into my cigar box—I felt I had an impression of maturity to convey.

"Hiya, Lieutenant."

"Still no sign of Frederick," he said, keeping his voice low. "And I haven't seen Heinz in the last couple of days either."

I was more concerned with a full report on the latest dirt about Miss Porter—but something told me that it just wasn't my business anymore.

Roth looked around the room uneasily. "We'd better come up with something soon." Then he asked if I would like to join him at the temple—he was on his way to say Kaddish for his father. "Maybe you'd like to say it for *your* dad," he suggested.

I told him I hadn't been to Hebrew school for weeks, even though my bar mitzvah was just around the corner. ". . . besides, I don't know what Kaddish means."

"Well, it's a special service that mourns the dead," Roth said. "On top of that, it's a prayer for the redemption and healing of suffering mankind." Obviously I looked intimidated, because he added, "It's really not that tough to learn, Zack."

It seemed like I'd done enough suffering to qualify, so I went into the kitchen and asked my mother if I could say Kaddish with Roth. She thought it was a "sweet idea," and with guilty eyes, confessed she hadn't attended any memorial services since my father's passing. "Say Kaddish for me too, Zachary."

On the way to Waterbury, Roth asked, "Have you started working on your bar mitzvah speech?"

"No."

"You know, besides the chanting and all the ritual," he said, "you're going to have to make a statement declaring how you intend to fulfill yourself as a man."

"I am?" Rabbi Glick had probably explained that, but a lot had been erased from my memory.

"Relax," Roth said. "When the time comes, I'll give you a hand."

I told him it would be simpler if I could just reuse *Roth's* bar mitzvah speech, but he shot down that idea. "By the way," he said, "I've arranged to have you placed under constant police protection right after the first of the year, and all through the trial.''

I swallowed uneasily. With Christmas and the holidays approaching, I'd somehow managed to forget I was mixed up in a murder case.

40

The big trial was due to start right after the holidays, about the same time school was to resume. With my mind preoccupied, it was tough to enjoy the festive season the way I had in previous years.

Thinking Coach Ryan must be lonely, I paid him another visit down at the jailhouse. Coincidently, Heinz's lawyer, a sinister man named Medwick, was there chatting to one of the deputies. Medwick, who reeked of Aqua Velva and looked like Peter Lorre, made a point of introducing himself to me. That, of course, got me wondering if he had any inkling that I was the sole witness to the killing. In any case, Ryan was in no mood for my company—even though I'd brought him a fresh supply of peanuts—so he told me to come back the next day. I could imagine how tough it must have been for Ryan to be spending Christmas in the tank; at the time though, I figured he was at least safe in the poky, which was more than I could say for myself.

Upon returning home, I found Lenny still grazing over his breakfast, and we got into a discussion about Oakville's lousy basketball season. Then, just as he started cracking some new Corky Pope jokes, the phone rang. For a change, I grabbed it first.

"Zack?" It was Miss Porter. She sounded distressed, and paused dramatically before blurting: "Heinz just told me you witnessed Greg's murder!"

"How'd he find that out?"

"I guess Pat Ryan told one of the deputies that as soon as you told your side of the story, he'd be free." She paused briefly. "Apparently, Ryan didn't realize the deputy was one of Heinz's men."

I was speechless. But it became clear to me why Ryan had acted so cool. He probably felt guilty.

"I don't know just how much you saw," Miss Porter said, "but I'm confident Heinz is going to make sure you don't tell anyone else."

I was still unable to speak.

"Zachary, please be careful." Lenny was standing closer, trying to get an earful.

"Thanks, Miss Porter," I said calmly, "I'll be careful." Hanging up, I tried to avoid Lenny's eyes.

"Careful about what?"

"She, uh, doesn't want me to play football . . . thinks I'll injure my drawing hand."

"Ain't that sweet."

I was in no mood for teasing, so I hurried out of the kitchen. As Lenny was mostly interested in my abandoned bagel and jam, I was able to make it to my bedroom without further abuse.

Pocketing my trusty Jack Armstrong Pedometer along with my Tom Mix Ranger Knife just in case, I set off for Heinz's house on Cooke Street. Coach Ryan had always preached: "The best defense is a bold offense." It was time to test that advice.

I figured the last place Heinz would search for me was in his own house. And while there, my hope was to turn up some valuable evidence. That was one thing Roth said you could never have enough of come trial time. The bottom line was, if I had stayed in the apartment I would've been trapped like a rat.

According to a previous pedometer reading—I kept an accurate list of distances to and from important places—Heinz's house was six-eighths of a mile from our apartment, which would take about eight minutes, walking.

The unpredictable New England weather had begun acting up, but it was still unseasonably warm. As I approached Heinz's house, a sudden wind blew the few remaining leaves from an old ash tree in the front yard. The driveway was empty, and so was the street.

A mangy black dog wandered over and sniffed my shoes. As he licked my hand, I patted his head. Then, the side door opened with a creak and Mrs. Heinz appeared. The mutt spotted her too, and took off. Mrs. Heinz glanced up and down the street, then strode off in the direction of town.

Gathering my courage, I moved toward the house. Assuming that both men were probably out hunting for me, I figured nobody would be home; I didn't know what I would do if Big Lew or Frederick happened to be inside, but I continued cautiously, holding my breath. Luckily, all was quiet as I stalked around back to check out the yard. Heinz kept a few hens in a little coop back there. They'd just been fed and I paused for a moment to watch them peck away. To this day I can't imagine Big Lew taking the time to toss his chickens some seed.

The battered door to the basement storage area was half open. So I poked my head inside. It was dark and quiet, and I entered slowly. Two rats scrambled out of a feed barrel and darted behind some boxes, like something out of a *Doc Savage* pulp. Tools and old equipment were neatly stored near the doorway. Picking up a tire iron, I advanced further. It was deathly quiet. The overhanging pipes were covered with spider webs which I brushed away with my free hand. And there was a nasty smell, like rotten fruit.

I noticed a door, moved to it and tried the knob. Locked. So I moved deeper inside, finding another door. I twisted the knob and this one gave way. I pushed open the door with my foot like all good movie detectives, then moved into a narrow, cluttered corridor. Half visible in the dim light was an old furnace, and next to that, several crates.

I moved in and out of the shadows slowly. Reaching the end of the corridor, I paused and listened. It was quiet. Spotting another door, I moved towards it, twisted the knob, then entered an eerie chamber which resembled some kind of shooting gallery. On the walls there were cut-out magazine pictures of all types of fighter planes and tanks, both U.S. and German. At the far end were at least fifty shattered bottles. The table in front of me was stacked with weapons, different sized pistols and rifles. Spent cartridges were scattered everywhere like peanut shells at a circus.

Picking up a rifle, I squinted to read the marking on the barrel, but it was too dark. If only I had sent off for that miniature Jack Armstrong Torpedo Flashlight advertised on the radio. As I started to move away, something dangling overhead struck my face. I reached up, flailing my arms. It was only a light-chain. I yanked it, and a dull yellow light came on.

The identification on the rifle read: .8 Mauser-

werke 98. I knew that was German. I had read about
the Mauser in *Life.* It was considered to be the most
deadly combat weapon ever made.

Suddenly there was a strange noise, and I wasn't
sure where it came from. I knew it wasn't the rats. It
sounded heavier, like a person shuffling. I waited a
minute. I couldn't contain my curiosity. Maybe there
was a Nazi hiding out here. Clutching the tire iron
tightly, I found myself advancing up the rickety stairs
and opening the door that led into the kitchen. Inside, the wooden cabinets were polished and gleam-
ing. The ancient refrigerator was spotless. It was
clear that if nothing else, at least Heinz's mother was
a tidy housekeeper.

I have no idea why, but I was overcome with an
urge to peek inside the fridge; there were a few beers,
some moldy cheese, various fruits and veggies, and a
juicy-looking glazed ham, which sat half-eaten on a
porcelain platter, with little plums. Pork was something one never found in our refrigerator, but something I'd always wanted to try. Smartly, I decided
"some other time."

I searched here and there, finally moving to the
hallway that led to the bedrooms. Mrs. Heinz's room
was open—at least I assumed it was hers. Then, I
eased open the door to the master bedroom and
stepped inside. It was obviously Big Lew's room.

The shades were drawn, the bed neatly made. It
was a large space, and Heinz kept a desk and wooden
filing cabinet in the corner. The walls were bare
except for a large map of Oakville and the neighbor-
ing vicinity tacked above the bed. Atop the cluttered
desk was a row of various beer mugs—just the sort of

thing you'd expect Big Lew to collect. Stacked underneath the biggest stein was a pile of nudie magazines. They were in French or some foreign language I couldn't read, but you didn't need words to understand the pictures. Big Lew was a bona fide pervert!

Then I heard that noise again. It sounded directly above me this time, maybe from the attic. But I had no intention of checking up there, knowing that wasn't the best place to get trapped.

Quickly shuffling through the stuff on Heinz's desk, I came across a small notebook—the record Heinz kept of people he'd been extorting money from. Among the familiar names, including Keller, I found "B. Silver" listed, with pencilled checkmarks indicating weekly payments going as far back as 1942. I was furious to think about all the pressures my father must have endured, and my grip tightened on the tire iron. Convinced Big Lew was indirectly responsible for my father's heart attack, I almost welcomed the idea of a confrontation.

Opening the file cabinet, I came across a folder labeled "Keller Plastic." Along with a couple of minor burglary reports, the file included a clipping reporting an accident that had occurred at the factory a few years previous, when a worker was killed unloading Phenol from a tank truck. Then I uncovered a memo to Heinz on Keller Plastic stationery that read: "This confirms our agreement to employ Carl Frederick as a chemical engineer at a starting salary of $200.00 per week, in lieu of security and protection payments henceforth." It was signed by Lewis Heinz and initialed by "S.K."

With the folder in hand, I hurried to get out of

there. But halfway out the door, I remembered what the lieutenant had said, that "evidence gained illegally was worthless." Frustrated, I returned and replaced the file before racing back out.

It wasn't until Heinz's house was a hundred yards behind me that I felt safe. Even then, it didn't take Dick Tracy to tell me that roaming the streets at night with Big Lew on the prowl was dangerous. But I had to contact Roth. So from a pay phone on Main Street, I tried reaching him at both the Waterbury Police Department and his home. No luck. Roth had made me promise never to call him again at the F.B.I.

Finally, I devised a plan I think even Jack Armstrong would've been proud of: I'd see what I could dig up at Keller Plastic on my own. And just in case I'd need Roth to come to my rescue, I prepared a package containing my pedometer and the following note: "I'm 7/8ths of mile from my apartment if you follow Jack Armstrong. Set for *my stride*. Go S/SW."

Dropping the parcel at the local police station, I told the deputy: "Lieutenant Roth is expecting this," figuring that if it got into the wrong hands at least they'd be thrown by the odd message. I could only hope that Roth would remember the length of my stride.

41

The liquor department at Silver's General flourished on New Year's Eve as the cash register jangled merrily. While my father was alive, we would celebrate the windfall with a trip to Waterbury that usually included a big dinner and a movie. The year my father died, I knew there wouldn't be any such treat, regardless of the business we did. Both Bailey and Lenny helped my mother out; luckily, the bowling alley was closed.

As the store was teeming with last minute shoppers, I was able to sneak away from the house undetected and make my way to Keller Plastic. The big factory—closed for the holiday—seemed like the perfect place to hide out. Besides, I had some snooping to do.

Considering the time of year, the night was mild, the sky filled with stars. Shortly it would be midnight, and the town was abuzz with anticipation. As was customary, gunshots and rockets would likely mark the arrival of 1946; which had always been a tradition in Oakville. But since this was the first peacetime New Year's since World War II, I doubted such a display would occur. Roth had said, though, that even after wars people still enjoyed firing guns—not necessarily at enemies—but in celebration.

Hiding behind a parked truck in the darkness, I studied the lone security guard at the loading platform. Pie-eyed, and clutching a half-empty whiskey bottle, he was listening to the annual broadcast of Guy Lombardo's Royal Canadians from the Waldorf. During wartime the plant had been heavily guarded, both inside and out. That New Year's Eve, security was the last thing on people's minds. From the look of the guard, he wouldn't have been much help anyway in the event of a break-in.

I could only assume that Roth had already picked up my package and with pedometer in hand, I could envision him striding to join me. Suddenly, a Buick drove up and skidded to a stop. A noisy couple emerged, each with a bottle in hand. I couldn't make out what they were saying—Lombardo was in the midst of "Rum and Coca-Cola"—though it appeared that the guard was being tempted into an early departure. Apparently an easy mark, he ducked inside the factory, switched off the exterior lights, then hurried back outside and hopped into the car. Before the car door even shut, they sped off in a chorus of laughter.

Piling a few crates under a small unlatched window I'd spotted, I climbed up, jimmied open the window with my Ranger Knife and squeezed through. I was becoming an expert at breaking and entering. Maibaum had mentioned that the factory had an alarm system, but luckily, nothing sounded. I closed the window behind me.

The last time I had been inside the factory was on a sixth grade field trip to witness Keller receiving a special defense citation. Afterwards, Keller, whose office atop a steel tier was accessible only by a single metal stairway, took the class on a plant tour. He boasted that all production was conducted under his watchful eye above the floor. The huge area below his office was filled with machinery, hydraulic presses, conveyer belts and numerous containers of raw chemicals.

The darkness was eerie, and I longed for that Torpedo Flashlight. Some light from the moon filtered in from the skylight, but the passing clouds made it sporadic at best. Bumping into one of the presses, I flashed back to the time Evette LaBeck's cousin had his hand dismembered in a factory accident. She'd brought the hospital medical pictures in for show and tell and I'd been unable to take my eyes off the grisly photos.

When I reached the center of the work area, I took a deep breath, then climbed the steps leading to Keller's office. At the top, I looked out over the rail and surveyed the entire plant.

As the door to Keller's office was ajar, I entered. Inside, the walls were covered with framed photographs, mostly of Keller and celebrities: Keller with one-armed baseball player Pete Gray of the St. Louis Browns; Keller with New York Governor Thomas E. Dewey, and Keller, Wentworth and Heinz at the opening of Waterbury's new City Hall. I got a kick out of Keller posing with Betty Grable at Grossinger's. He was smiling slyly, his eyes riveted on Grable's gams.

The adjacent office contained a secretary's desk and two large file cabinets. I popped on the desk lamp, slid open the file drawer labeled D-G and fished through the folders. Removing Frederick's file, I placed it on the desk and started my search. A standard work application indicated that Frederick, not yet naturalized, was born in Austria in 1910 and educated at Heidelberg with a degree in chemical engineering. I was more than surprised to see his U.S. sponsor listed as Mary Beth Porter.

As I replaced the file, I wondered what was keeping Roth. Had he screwed up trying to maintain my twenty five-inch stride? Or was he expecting me to be outside? Suddenly there was a loud clunk, like a huge door slamming shut. I rushed onto the platform. Straining to see in the dark, I shouted: "I'm up here!" I waved my arms back and forth. "Lieutenant!"

There was a moment of silence before I realized I'd made a grave mistake. The silhouetted figure that stepped into the stream of moonlight below was much larger than Roth. In fact, it was Big Lew. Needless to say, I nearly fainted dead away. I couldn't fathom how he had tracked me down, until it occurred to me that a silent alarm might have been directly connected to the police station.

My first concern was what method Big Lew would use to kill me. Knife? Gun? Or would he keep it clean and stick with strangulation? Before I could even consider all the possibilities, Heinz grabbed a length of heavy chain from a workbench and started up the stairs.

I'm not sure what inspired me, but like Batman, I sprang over the platform rail and hurtled down, crashing onto boxes and a rack of shelves. Bottles and beakers went flying, glass shattering everywhere. A thick blue liquid oozed over the floor. Lurching up to run, I felt a sharp pain. It was the same damned ankle I'd sprained the year before playing football.

In his pursuit, Big Lew slipped on the blue slime and went down hard. I heard his head smack the concrete floor, followed by groans. Seizing the chance, I gathered my strength and dashed across the floor. I felt like Glenn Davis in an Army game. And I climaxed the sprint by sliding beneath a large press. Hiding behind some crates and chemical vats, I tried desperately to remember where the main door was located. Even though Big Lew was wounded, I just knew he would recover before I could escape.

The way I saw it, I had two choices: either stay put and hope he couldn't find me or make a break for the nearest wall and follow it around the building until I found an exit. Hiding out seemed less risky, but I knew how enraged Big Lew would be after smashing his head. If he did manage to find me, I was like a sitting duck. So I burst from my lair and raced towards the wall.

I noticed the sliding door at the loading dock, and sprinted in that direction, all the while too scared to so much as glance behind me. I pushed with all my strength, but it became painfully clear that the door wasn't going to budge.

"Looks like you didn't eat your Wheaties this morning, Silver!"

I swung around to find Big Lew making a beeline for my neck. In the moonglow I could see how his head was bashed and how the left side of his face was smeared with blood. But that didn't keep him from grinning madly.

"ZACHARY! WHERE ARE YOU?"

Thank God, it was Roth—but I couldn't spot him in the darkness. It stopped Big Lew momentarily though, and as he turned to confront the lieutenant, it bought me enough time to spot an "Emergency" doorway nearby and slip outside. That set off an alarm, and it blared.

Hobbling across the parking lot toward Smith's Pond, I figured I'd finally escaped, assuming that Roth had captured and arrested Big Lew. But as I turned back to catch my breath, I noticed only one figure emerge from the plant. With the chain clutched in his fist, Big Lew was still dogging me.

42

The moon was hidden behind the clouds, making the night dark and gloomy. Plodding through the slush up the bank towards the pond, I couldn't understand why Roth hadn't plugged Big Lew with his .38. Then I had a terrible thought: what if Big Lew had finished Roth off with that chain?

Pausing to inspect my throbbing ankle, I discovered that it had swollen to twice its normal size. Big Lew was a bloody mess but that didn't even slow him down. He just kept moving forward, no doubt driven by his rage to slaughter me.

As I reached the edge of the frozen-over pond I heard shots. At first I thought Roth had finally come to the rescue. But when more bursts sounded, I realized it was only that midnight and the New Year had arrived. A spectacular rocket burst overhead, all red, white and blue. The whole town was celebrating—everyone except me, that is.

I could hardly see in the darkness, and I slipped and skidded on the frozen surface as I ran. Not only had kids thrown rocks and junk on the ice, but several broken tree stumps were jutting up through the crust like jagged spears. Despite Big Lew right behind me, my fear turned towards falling through the ice and I started having visions of the day Peewee Morse fell through. It had happened shortly after my father forbade me to skate unless the temperature ran below zero for at least a week. Buddy and I were on the pond that day with Peewee, and all I could think about then was how much hell I'd catch if my father found out I was skating before I was supposed to. So the minute Peewee went under, I took off. I didn't learn that he had drowned until later that night when Buddy called. I always felt guilty for leaving so quickly.

It wasn't particularly cold although my body was drenched in sweat. There was a small, sheltered cove at the far end of the pond and I headed in that direction. But I caught my bad foot on a rock and went flying, landing with a thump and sliding to a stop. As I lay there, cold and soaking, I heard the ice beneath me rumble and shake. There was a low, echoing clack, as though the entire pond was about to crack and give way. I held my breath, not moving a muscle. But Big Lew would soon be upon me, and I knew I had to do something—fast.

Reaching into my pants pocket, I withdrew my trusty Ranger Knife. I opened the blade, and stretching out flat, started scratching and chipping the ice in a line about three feet across—hoping with all my might to coax Big Lew over the scored spot.

I could only think this was the end of my life as I frantically chipped away. And I recalled hearing how at the very moment before death, a person's whole life flashes before their eyes—but nothing was happening to me yet. It was still dark and despite the chill, I got this strange craving for one of my father's ice cream sundaes—the kind he used to make just for me. Then finally, the flashes started: I saw myself dancing with Miss Porter at our wedding as Rabbi Glick watched disapprovingly because I'd married outside the faith. What followed was a parade of all my dreams and fantasies, like being the first Jewish player to score fifty points in the Garden. Sobbing and frustrated, I hacked madly at the ice. Then, suddenly, the knife blade folded into the sheath and sliced into my hand. I yelped in pain as the blood started spilling. Grabbing my hanky, I wrapped it tight around my fist and tried to control my whimpering.

"I can hear you!" Big Lew shouted.

"ROTTHHHHH!" My desperate cry disappeared in the darkness.

Big Lew reacted immediately. "I'm gonna shut you up for good, Jewboy!"

In the distance, I spotted Big Lew's silhouette, sliding as he ran, swinging his chain like a lasso. Though he was still fifty yards away, I could hear him panting. Gathering my wits, I pulled myself to my knees and crawled behind an enormous dead tree that had fallen into the pond, half-submerged in the ice. I couldn't run anymore. My legs were cramped up from the cold and the fear began constricting my throat, causing a choking sensation. Every move I made became sluggish and painful. It was as though my body had already surrendered. I clutched a jagged limb with my good hand, my swollen ankle with the other, and watched in terror as Big Lew headed toward me.

I closed my eyes and uttered something I'd learned in Hebrew school: "Beyodo afkid ruhi, beith ishan veoiroh. Hashem li velo iroh . . ." I chanted it just loud enough to lure Big Lew over the spot I had chipped.

"Prayers won't help you, stupid Jew!"

I kept my eyes tightly closed. I didn't want to see that chain when it came down on my head. But I could hear Big Lew gasping. He was no more than twelve feet away, so I braced myself for the first blow, praying that after that I'd lose consciousness.

But instead of the whoosh of a chain, I heard that terrible rumble and cracking sound again, this time more violent. My eyes popped open and I saw Big Lew just as the ice broke open beneath him. He had a look of mortal fear—an expression I'll never forget. A second later he was swallowed up by the cold, polluted water.

I watched, astounded, clinging to the half-buried tree for support. A smattering of bubbles emerged from under the huge chunks of floating ice. The water and ice buckled and rippled beneath me, but didn't give way. I closed my eyes, finding sanctuary in the silence.

Crack!

A fist smashed through the ice inches away, still clutching one end of the chain. I grabbed the tree tighter, looked into the sky, and shouted my prayer this time.

After an interminable moment, Big Lew's hand slipped quietly into the water. The moon crept back from behind the clouds and a dull glow shimmered on the ice. It was 1946. The war was over. I was alive, and all I could do was cry. The more I cried, the better I felt. Only now, the pain in my hand resumed.

I don't how long I was staring down at the gaping hole in the ice before I heard Roth call my name. At first I thought I was dreaming. Then I saw him emerge from the darkness of the shore and hurry towards me.

"Zack! You all right, Zack?"

I nodded, still clinging to the tree as Roth circled the opening in the ice, inching closer.

"Get back," he barked, realizing what had happened to Big Lew.

I let go of the tree and took a small step away. Then suddenly, without warning, the lieutenant plunged into the dark frigid water, clothes and all. He disappeared out of sight beneath the chunks of ice amidst splashing and thrashing and thousands of bubbles.

Shortly the water started to calm and the bubbling stopped, leaving the surface black and ominous. It was during those silent seconds, while I stared down at the water, that I understood how much I really cared for Roth.

Suddenly, two heads burst to the surface. Roth had Big Lew by the hair. He was still alive, gasping and struggling. As he lunged for Roth's throat, the lieutenant clipped him hard on the jaw, causing Big Lew's head to flop sideways, his mouth agape.

I quickly flipped onto my stomach and extended my good arm as far as I could reach. Roth took hold, pulled himself and Big Lew to the frozen edge and hoisted his limp body onto the ice.

"What the heck did you do that for?" I demanded.

Roth, breathing heavily, was still in total control. "I want to bring him to justice . . . It's better that way."

"Better for who?"

Roth looked at me solemnly, his watery eyes blinking. "He's a man, Zack . . . same as you and me."

As we made our way toward the bank, I watched Roth lugging Big Lew by the collar. It was too much for me to comprehend.

43

I couldn't stop shivering. I realized how close to death I'd actually been, and my body was reacting to the shock. "Big Lew was coming at me with a chain, and the ice opened right up," I babbled, still dazed.

"Tell me later," Roth said. "First, we've got to get you to the hospital. You're going to need a couple of stitches in that hand."

But I couldn't contain myself. My head was spinning with all the details and the jabbering was helping to settle me down. "Then when Big Lew came back up through the ice I thought I was a goner."

As Roth helped me into the car, I noticed the F.B.I. backup men, who had appeared from nowhere, handcuff Big Lew, then heave him into a sedan and whisk him away.

Driving back through the deserted streets, Roth explained why he hadn't fired at Big Lew in the factory. "I couldn't take the chance of hitting you. It was too dark."

I thought of his gimpy hand, and I was glad he hadn't tried.

"Actually, I didn't think I was ever going to find you," he said. "With your damn twenty-five inch stride, I might as well have crawled across town."

I smiled for the first time that night, picturing Roth taking kid steps all the way down Main Street.

"People in Oakville already think I'm a little strange," Roth said. "And my walk over here didn't exactly help my image. You should've seen the look I was getting.''

''What about Frederick?''

Roth paused, then smiled with satisfaction. "We got 'im. He's locked up.''

I shouted triumphantly. We clasped hands and embraced affectionately, almost causing Roth to swerve into a roadside tree.

''Frederick was hiding out in Heinz's attic,'' he said.

''So those were the noises,'' I muttered to myself. ''They had it all fixed up very comfortably,'' he continued. ''We even grabbed Mrs. Heinz on accessory charges. You should have heard her squawking.''

I grinned, thrilled I wouldn't be subjected to her sour mug around town anymore. ''But I still don't get it. Why was Big Lew helping the Nazi out?''

''Frederick is better known as Karl Friedrich Heinzmann, Heinz's older brother,'' Roth explained. ''Heinzmann was a top-ranking Nazi officer. His area of expertise was poison gas used in the extermination camps.'' Roth gave a deep sigh. ''We've been after Herr Heinzmann for over a year now, but the identification change was causing us problems.''

I wasn't that shocked about Frederick's relationship to Big Lew, but I never dreamed he'd be such a plum for the F.B.I. The pieces were all falling into place and I had this strange feeling that it had all happened before. I guess those radio crime dramas left me expecting a similar ending, where the good guys won and the bad guys went to prison. If it had turned out differently, I would have been disappointed.

"That's why they sent me to hunt for him in Brazil," Roth said. "When I got back to the States, we got wind of allegations that Heinz was trying to organize the K.K.K. in Roxbury. There was also Pat Ryan's phone call claiming a Nazi officer was living in Oakville that got us thinking. Then, when Heinz was implicated in the Bondi murder, I asked to be put on the case. With Heinz's badge suspended, it was a perfect chance to investigate."

"But how did you know Big Lew and Frederick were related?"

"I didn't. All we knew was that they might be connected in some way because someone in Oakville, using Miss Porter's name, sponsored Frederick's move into the U.S. That was our only lead. Eventually, Mary Beth told me that Heinz was blackmailing her. Then, everything made sense."

Looking back now, it still intrigues me that both Heinzmann and Rothstein changed their names to hide their identities—one a villain, the other a hero. I tried to digest all the facts and sort out the details, but I couldn't. It didn't really matter anyway. Heinz and Frederick had finally been put away and that was the important thing. For the first time since the murder, I felt perfectly safe. But curiously, I was still trembling.

"I've been thinking," I said. "Do I still have to testify?"

"Yes," Roth said. "It's your responsibility."

This didn't stop my trembling. But after thinking it over for a moment, I knew it was the right thing to do. Besides, two weeks later I was officially going to become a "man."

As we turned onto Main Street the first thing I

noticed were the Christmas lights blinking in our store window. Everything looked exactly the same, which surprised me a little. I was almost expecting things to be visibly different already. What with Big Lew out of action, I'd hoped Oakville might finally be the "perfect town" my mother always spoke of—a place where "only nice people live and nothing bad ever happens." But the only thing that had changed was me.

44

Standing before my family and friends at the Temple
Beth Zion in my blue suit, new tie and dress shoes, I
was finally about to deliver my bar mitzvah speech.
Though healing nicely, my wound was still bandaged
and conveniently served as a reminder to everyone of
my recent ordeal—and heroics. Considering what
had been packed into the twelve years I was leaving
behind, I felt confidently mature.

I'd already destroyed the lipstick-stained cigarette I
had been harboring for the past several weeks since it
turned out that Miss Porter had nothing to do with
the killing. And by now, I was confident the man at
the Christmas Party was not Roth. I'd noticed the
looks between Miss Porter and Murphy in the hall-
ways at Baldwin, and she was obviously in love.

Gazing down at my mother and Lenny sitting together in the front row, I finally felt that they were
looking at me as an adult. Lenny had this half-smirk
that said: "I hate to admit it kid, but I'm proud as
hell." My mother, as lovely as ever in a pretty new
dress, looked like she'd been crying all morning—she
knew how much my father wanted to see his youngest son at his bar mitzvah. Buddy and Melissa were
also seated in the first row, next to Maibaum. Behind
them were Birdwell and Popovich and a few other
classmates. Birdwell fiddled self-consciously with his
yarmulke, while Popovich, in a clean sweater for a

change, looked as though he'd at least had a bath and combed his hair for the occasion.

Unfortunately, Roth was absent. He was on assignment in Germany, having personally escorted Frederick to Nuremberg to be tried with all the other high-ranking Nazis for their crimes.

Big Lew's murder trial had come and gone, and my testimony was the key to his conviction—forever ending Heinz's reign of terror in Oakville. As promised, Roth stood by me throughout the ordeal. He even helped me with my bar mitzvah speech.

"But the main thing," Roth had said, "is to accept the responsibility of manhood, and to be honest." Before leaving for the airport, he said, "Don't forget, we're going to Madison Square Garden as soon as I get back." Most of all though, I knew I'd never forget the restraint and compassion Roth had shown with Big Lew.

The synagogue was bathed in a warm golden light as I took a long look around. No one was more surprised than I was to spot Miss Porter, looking gorgeous in a taffeta dress, appear in back carrying a small wrapped package. I remember myself thinking, "Please, God, don't let it be another art book!" Cezanne's cubism still had me baffled; I guess I'd be permanently affected. Then, for a brief but wonderful moment, our eyes met and she gave me a reassuring wink. Such a simple wink—but for me, it defined our new relationship. And I felt good.

Clearing my throat, I began. "My beloved mother, dear brother Leonard, Rabbi Glick and good friends . . . today I am a man."

Acknowledgments

I would like to thank Brent V. Friedman, Joseph Manduke, Steven Pressfield, Alan Berger and my children, Jonathan and Gabrielle for their generous help and encouragement.

E.P.

Temple Israel

Minneapolis, Minnesota

IN HONOR OF THE BAR MITZVAH OF
JACOB MEYER GREENE
FROM
HIS FAMILY

NOVEMBER 7, 1992